THE DRAGON MISTRESS:
BOOK 1

Other books by R. A. Steffan

The Complete Horse Mistress Collection
The Complete Lion Mistress Collection
The Complete Dragon Mistress Collection
The Complete Master of Hounds Collection

Her Band of Rakes: A Regency Reverse Harem

*Secret Pack: The Complete Trilogy (RH
Omegaverse, written as Ember Blaze)*

Circle of Blood: Books 1-3
Circle of Blood: Books 4-6
The Last Vampire: Books 1-3
The Last Vampire: Books 4-6
(with Jaelynn Woolf)

Vampire Bound: Complete Series, Books 1-4

Forsaken Fae: The Complete Series, Books 1-3

The Sixth Demon: Book One
The Sixth Demon: Book Two

Antidote: Love and War, Book 1
Antigen: Love and War, Book 2
Antibody: Love and War, Book 3
Anthelion: Love and War, Book 4
Antagonist: Love and War, Book 5

THE DRAGON MISTRESS:
BOOK 1

R. A. STEFFAN

The Dragon Mistress: Book 1

ISBN: 978-1-955073-54-7 (paperback)

For information, contact the author at
http://www.rasteffan.com/contact/

Cover art by Deranged Doctor Design

Second Edition: May 2022

Author's Note

This book contains descriptions of graphic sex and violence. It is intended for a mature audience.

TABLE OF CONTENTS

ONE

"I can't believe those bastards stole my horse. Damn it, I *liked* that horse."

The sun blazed above me, unmoved by my lament. I knew, deep down, that my lost horse should not have been my first concern. Lying bruised and beaten by the side of the road as I was—with no food, no water, and punishing heat beating down on my aching head—the loss of the weedy little chestnut mare I'd purchased in the port town of Adumine was the least of my worries.

Stop whining, Frella. It could have been worse, I tried to tell myself.

I'd done my best to fight off the bandits when they rode up and surrounded us, but there were four of them, and the pair of no-good cheats I'd been traveling with had obviously been in on the whole thing from the start—leading me straight into a trap.

I only had two throwing knives on me. One had stuck in a bandit's leather chest armor, failing to penetrate the flesh beneath. The other knife found the meat of a second man's thigh, but he'd only yanked it out, cursing, and charged at me on horseback, knocking me from Laduna's saddle.

The fall stunned me, and I was easy prey after that. The one with the leather armor grabbed me and held me against his broad chest. A meaty hand covered my mouth as I kicked and struggled fruitlessly, trying without success to get any kind of leverage to use against him. He was wearing sturdy half-gloves, so I couldn't even bite him. His tall, heavy boots meant my attempts to kick his shins or stomp on his toes only made him twist one of my arms painfully behind my back.

"Check her saddlebags," my captor snapped in Utrean. "She's foreign, but she's got money—that's clear enough."

The man and woman who'd been riding with me went to catch Laduna, while the other three bandits loitered nearby, leering at me. I could feel my temper rising. That was a bad sign, I knew. Ithric and Keenan had spent years trying to teach me to stay calm during a fight rather than let my emotions carry me away. The lessons never stuck, unfortunately—and I knew full well why that was, even if I'd never told them in so many words.

I got angry because anger was better than fear.

That was why I started flailing like a madwoman in the leader's grip—shrieking against the hand muffling my face as the man I'd injured came limping up and grabbed my breast in one blood-soaked paw.

"I'll teach you a lesson, bitch," he said, easily dodging my feet as I kicked out. His hand squeezed painfully, and I wrenched against the grip on my arm that threatened to tear something in my shoulder if I continued to struggle.

"We can take turns with her," said another of the onlookers, his voice high-pitched and sniveling. "I ain't never seen hair that color before. It's almost like gold. You think it's the same color down below?"

The fingers that had been digging into my breast moved to squeeze roughly between my legs, and I screamed again—in rage, I assured myself. A roar of rage—the sound mostly muffled by the hand covering my mouth. My heart pounded against my ribs—*also in rage*, godsdamnit. I bucked, trying to dislodge the hands even if I dislocated my shoulder in the process.

"Sounds like you're about to regret throwing those knives in a very big way, little peach," the man holding me said, not even sounding out of breath from containing my struggles. *Smug bastard.*

My tunic was made of the light, flowing material favored for travel in the arid uplands east of the coastal port. I regretted that fact as Grabby Hands took hold of the collar and tore it open, ripping it nearly to my navel. Still, the distraction was enough for one of my flailing feet to catch him sharply in the knee, on the same leg I'd pierced earlier with the blade.

He grunted, and the answering fist to my stomach would have doubled me over if Leather Armor hadn't been holding me upright. I fought the urge to empty my stomach contents. Not only would doing so hurt my aching gut even more—it would also be really, really disgusting, considering Leather Armor's left hand was still clapped over my mouth.

"Oy!" called one of the two-timing bastards who'd gone after my horse. "Look over there!"

Everyone turned to look in the direction I'd come from. Unfortunately, Leather Armor's tight hold on me — not to mention the tears of pain in my eyes — meant that I couldn't see whatever had caused the commotion.

"Son of a poxy whore," Sniveling Voice cursed. "What're the odds? Anything good in those saddlebags, Midhan?"

"Yes, there's food and money," the woman said. "Some fancy clothing that might fetch a bit, too."

I tried to crane around and glare at her. What kind of woman stood by while another woman was assaulted by a gang of men? The criminal kind, I supposed, and mentally kicked myself for trusting her and her crooked partner.

"*Shit.* Stupid bitch!" Grabby Hands snarled. "No time for fun. Let's just kill her, and fucking *go.*" He smacked my exposed breast *hard*, startling a muffled yelp from me.

An *angry* yelp. Not a girly one. The yelp of someone who was really, really pissed off, and not scared out of her wits in the least.

Leather Armor's hand fell away from my mouth, in favor of patting me down roughly. In moments, he found the small but heavy coin purse hanging from my belt and yanked it free.

"Nah," he said. "Just leave her. What's she gonna do with no food, water, or money? It's bad luck to kill a woman."

He gave me a shove and I staggered free, whirling to face him, my mouth hanging open in outrage. "Wait. You were all ready to gang rape me, but killing me would be *bad luck*? Seriously—*what the actual fuck?*"

I did mention about my temper, didn't I?

The gloved fist that flashed toward my face an instant before pain exploded in my right cheekbone probably shouldn't have come as a surprise. But—not gonna lie, here—the impact as I slammed face-first into the rocky ground, head reeling... well. It *was* kind of surprising. I rolled over, spitting out sandy grit, only vaguely aware of the others mounting up and leaving with Laduna in tow as my consciousness wavered in and out.

And that's how I found myself lying bruised and battered by the side of the road with no food, no water, no transportation, and my exposed tits slowly turning red under the unforgiving rays of the desert sun. So... *yeah.* Laduna's theft maybe shouldn't have been my biggest concern at that particular point in time.

It also wasn't the best time to realize that, finally, after almost a dozen years of trying, I'd had a real adventure. And, so far? Adventure sucked donkey cock.

That was certainly disappointing.

I sighed. Assuming I didn't die of heat stroke right here in the middle of the Utrean desert, I was never breathing a single word of this to Keenan, Ithric, my brother, my guardians back in Draebard, or anyone else. The sky spun in slow circles above me, making me queasy. I closed my eyes against the sight.

Just for a moment, I promised. *I'll just rest here for a moment, until I get my breath back, that's all.* My last thought, before darkness snuck across my mind with stealthy cat's feet, was to wonder what the men had seen in the distance earlier to make them leave.

⌁ ♕ ⌁

I blinked, my eyes feeling as gritty as the sand that surrounded me. The hazy blob hovering above me solidified into a face. Large. Male. Heavy-featured. What I'd taken for shadows from being backlit was actually skin so dark it looked like polished ebony. Huh. That was strange. Not to mention quite strikingly attractive. I'd never see anyone with skin so dark before. I blinked.

Wait. Big, male, and looming over me?

My heart kicked into life, pounding hard against the walls of my chest. Everything hurt, but I still clenched a fist and swung it toward the man's throat, hoping for a quick takedown.

Surprise flared in eyes so black I couldn't see where the pupil ended and the iris began. He jerked a shoulder up to block me, damn him—the movement so fast that my blow rolled off hard muscle instead of bruising a soft windpipe.

"Whoa!" he said, but I was already scrabbling backward, trying to gain enough space to roll to my feet; hoping dizziness wouldn't send me right back down again.

To my surprise, rather than press his advantage, the man stepped back with his hands raised in a gesture of peace that was almost comical, given his height and massive, muscular frame. A male laugh from somewhere nearby drew my attention, though my balance threatened to desert me when I started to turn. I staggered, but kept my feet.

The laugh was light and clear, nothing like the cruel amusement of the bandits. "Eldris, my friend," said the laugh's owner. "You look like you went to stroke a sweet little pussy in the granary and discovered a crouched panther instead!"

I had a confused impression of gray eyes the color of a finely honed steel blade, and long, mahogany-colored hair with a single streak of white running through it. Then my attention was jerked back to the dark-skinned man in front of me, who harrumphed.

"No one wants to hurt you, all right?" he said, still holding his hands palm-out. "I was just checking to see how bad you were injured, that's all."

At that point, I realized several things in quick succession. First, my tongue felt like it had swollen until there was hardly enough room for it in my mouth. Second, there were four people arrayed around me, not just two. In addition to the dark man and the one on horseback who had laughed at me, a woman and another man were mounted nearby. The other man held two additional horses—one saddled for riding and the other carrying loaded panniers.

The next thing I realized—and perhaps the most important thing so far—was that my ripped tunic still gaped open, leaving one of my breasts half-covered and the other one hanging out for everyone to see. *Charming.* I fumbled for the light material, pulling it together as best I could.

"Water?" I rasped, fighting my swollen tongue. Swallowing my pride would have been a whole lot easier if my throat weren't so dry.

The woman had been watching, wide-eyed, from the back of her petite gray horse. She was straight-backed and willowy—effortlessly elegant in a way I never had been and never would be. She had the thick black hair, brown eyes and olive-tinted skin common amongst her countrymen. She was dressed very finely and had an air of delicacy about her that made me think she was from a rich family. Perhaps even nobility.

Now, concern appeared to break her free of her earlier paralysis. "Of course! I'm so terribly sorry for staring," she said in a sweet, lilting voice. "Aristede, please be so good as to get this poor young woman a drink."

"Just try to stay out of punching range while you do it," said the third man—the one holding the horses. His tone was as dry as the desert landscape around us.

The man with the white streak in his long, brown hair—Aristede by name, apparently—snorted in amusement and dismounted, unhooking a waterskin from his saddle. The pull of water was like a lodestone drawing me toward him. He smiled and held out the skin. It was a nice smile, and one I might have been able to appreciate more if I could have torn my eyes away from the water.

"There you go," he said, as I took the water. "Help yourself. We're well-provisioned, and we're only a day or so out from Safaad."

The water was stale, lukewarm, and quite possibly the best thing I had ever tasted. When my thirst was slaked, I resisted the urge to pour some of the remaining contents over my head and arms. That might have been acceptable back home on the island of Eburos, but I'd seen enough to know that water was precious in the Utrean uplands.

"Thank you," I managed, sounding more like myself. I was still bruised and aching, but the dizziness was receding and my vision no longer wavered.

"What on earth happened to you, you poor thing?" the woman asked. "We saw the plume of dust from several riders, but we were too far away to make out any details."

I wiped my mouth with the back of my hand and corked the waterskin before reluctantly handing it back. "I was set upon by bandits. They stole my horse and all my belongings." Just saying the words made the anger flare in my belly once more.

The dark-skinned giant—Eldris—gave my torn tunic a pointed look. "Seems like they were after more than your horse and your supplies." His expression was stony.

The woman made a noise of dismay. I gritted my teeth, not having any particular desire to discuss it.

"Yeah. Well, you said you saw the dust rising from their horses' hooves. I guess they saw the dust rising from yours, too. I think that's what convinced them to leave."

"Thank goodness for that," said the woman. "But still—how horrible for you to have gone through such a thing! You must allow us to escort you the rest of the way to Safaad. It's far too difficult a journey on foot."

I wasn't about to pass up that offer. "Thank you," I said, with unfeigned relief. "I think you four may have just saved my life."

"Don't give it a second thought," my sweet-natured savior insisted. "I'm only sorry we didn't arrive sooner. Now, forgive my manners. My name is Gladya. This is Eldris, and Aristede." She gestured to the dark-skinned man and the man who'd given me the water, confirming the names I'd already mentally applied to them. "And this is Rayth." She waved toward the man who was still mounted. Rayth dipped his chin a fraction, but said nothing.

"I'm Frella of Draebard," I told them. "To say that I'm pleased to make your acquaintance is an understatement, believe me."

They all smiled except for Rayth.

Aristede cocked his head. "Draebard, eh? I've not heard of it. Is that up north somewhere?"

"*Way* up north," I told him. "On the Isle of Eburos."

"Ah," he said. "That's quite a journey from here. And it would explain your..." He trailed off, gesturing at his hair in a way that indicated my fair coloring.

"Interesting," Eldris said. "Are there lots of people with blue eyes and honey-colored hair in the northern lands? I've never seen hair that light before."

We studied each other shamelessly for a moment. "It's not uncommon," I said. "Don't feel bad, though. I've never seen someone with ebony skin before. Where are you from?"

"Kulawi," he said. "It's also quite a way from here. Right across the Great Southern Desert."

"Sorry, never heard of it," I admitted.

The flash of white teeth he gave me had a guarded edge to it. "Maybe just as well," he said. "Most people are scared when I tell them that."

"Oh?" I asked.

"The Kulawi people have a reputation for ferocity," Aristede offered.

"For being brutes, you mean," Eldris said, and there was a hint of long-buried bitterness lurking behind the words. "People 'round here consider us savages."

I couldn't help it—I laughed. Eldris' eyes narrowed, but I just shook my head. "Sorry," I said. "It's just that a lot of people on the continent consider the Eburosi to be barbarians." I stepped forward and stretched a hand out. "As one barbarian savage to another, I'm pleased to make your acquaintance. Apologies for the attempted throat-punching thing, by the way."

His hard expression melted into a smile that transformed his whole face. He clasped me forearm to forearm, his grip firm but not punishing. "Barbarian, eh? I like that. Pleased to meet you, too." He let go, and made a vague gesture toward my torso. "And, uh, your tits are hanging out again. Thought you might want to know."

"Crap." I clutched at the torn tunic, feeling my traitorous northern skin flush with embarrassed heat. At least the sunburn would keep it from being as noticeable to the others. Probably.

Gladya dismounted and led her gray over to the packhorse, where she rummaged through one of the panniers. "Let me get you something to wear. I'm afraid what you're wearing now is a bit beyond help."

She pulled out a silky length of ivory-colored cloth and handed it to me with a hesitant smile.

"Thank you," I said with feeling. Modesty seemed a bit ridiculous since I'd already flashed all of them more than once, so I just turned my back and quickly stripped off the ruined tunic, replacing it with the borrowed one.

It was too snug in places—Gladya was a tall, slender woman, and I was all short, plump curves that never seemed to diminish no matter how hard or strong the muscles underneath grew. Beggars couldn't be choosers, though, unless I wanted to try to borrow a shirt from one of the men.

I turned around, and could have sworn I saw Aristede staring at my slightly squished cleavage before he dragged his eyes back to my face and pasted on a pleasant expression.

"We should leave," Rayth said. "An extra rider will slow us down, and we've lingered here long enough as it is."

Oh? Sorry I messed up your carefully laid itinerary, Sunshine, I thought, though fortunately I had regained enough presence of mind by that point not to say it aloud.

"I'm game," I said aloud. "How do you want to do this?"

Rayth gave the group a quick once-over. "Ride with Aristede. His horse can carry two. If the mare starts to flag, I'll take you for a bit."

Ride with Rayth? *Be still my heart.* Hopefully, Aristede's mare wouldn't flag. I resolved to think light and airy thoughts.

"Fine by me," I told him. "Aristede?"

"It would be my pleasure," he assured me. He returned the half-empty waterskin he'd offered me to its place at the front of his saddle and offered Gladya a bent knee to use as a mounting aid. She climbed delicately onto the little gray horse and flashed me an encouraging smile. From the corner of my eye, I saw Eldris mount his sturdy chestnut gelding.

Aristede gestured at his rather magnificent bay mare, offering me a leg up. I waved him off.

"You first," I said. "If you'll lend me an arm, I can swing up behind you."

He shrugged agreement and lifted himself smoothly into the saddle. Leaning down a bit, he proffered a bent elbow. I grasped it, taking two quick steps and forcing overtaxed muscles to spring, pivoting my body around the fulcrum of his strong arm to swing my leg up and over. He lifted at the same time I jumped, and I settled into place behind him with only a bit of shifting and scooting to center myself.

"Impressive," he said, sounding amused. "Do all northern barbarians learn how to leap onto horses' backs like that as a matter of course?"

I snorted and wrapped an arm around his stomach, not above taking a moment to appreciate the firm body in front of me. He'd made vaulting up here easy, using exactly the right timing and amount of force to help me.

"Only the ones who were raised by a village Horse Mistress, I'm afraid. Honestly, in most clans on Eburos, women don't ride or work much with animals. It's, um, kind of a cultural thing."

A *stupid* cultural thing, I didn't add.

"Oh, I'd hate to be reliant on wagons or riding with a man to get from place to place," Gladya said. "Good for you and your Horse Mistress for ignoring such a silly rule!"

I nodded. "I was relieved when I got to Adumine, and found that no one blinked an eye at selling me a horse." The reminder of Laduna, my little chestnut mare, brought the simmering anger in my gut back to a boil. "I still can't *believe* those no good bastards stole her. I swear to the gods, I'm going to track them down and make them pay. I'll get that mare back if it's the last thing I do."

I realized that I was squeezing Aristede a little tighter than was probably polite, though he'd uttered no complaint. I eased off, feeling a bit sheepish.

"And how, exactly, do you propose to undertake your righteous crusade?" Rayth said with the air of dismissiveness that I was already coming to loathe. "The bandits have a significant head start on us, and will have sold your horse and belongings before we ever reach Safaad. Once they do, they'll be gone like smoke on the wind."

Damn him—it's not like I'd asked anyone to bring logic into the discussion.

"I'll figure something out," I said, biting off the words.

"What in the name of sanity were you doing traveling from Adumine to Safaad alone in the first place?" Rayth asked, and he didn't have to finish with the words *you idiot woman* for me to hear them loud and clear.

"I wasn't traveling alone," I snapped. "The caravan I was supposed to travel with canceled at the last moment. The ship carrying the goods they'd planned to transport sank off the coast. I eventually found a man and a woman who were heading this way and who agreed to take me." My lips twisted. "Unfortunately, they apparently make their living by leading unsuspecting travelers right into bandits' hands in exchange for a cut of the spoils."

Aristede grunted in distaste. "That's unfortunate. Do you remember anything distinguishing about the bandits?" he asked, rather more practically.

I silently thanked him for moving the conversation away from my humiliating exercise in poor judgment. "I could describe the couple I was riding with in detail. The man went by the name Omerah, and the woman was called Midhan." I went on to describe the four men who had set upon me as best I could.

Eldris grunted. "Nothing out of the ordinary in any of that, sad to say."

"And both Omerah and Midhan are fairly common names near the coast," Gladya added. "What about their horses?"

"Also common," I said. "No unusual markings, and not highly bred or particularly well cared for. Their tack was old and not very good quality." I flashed back to Grabby Hands charging at me on his plain chestnut gelding after I'd skewered his leg. "One of them did have an odd marking embroidered on the corner of his saddle cloth. It was faded, but it looked like a triangle with a line extending out from each of the three corners, and the lines ended in identical spirals. It was done in dark thread, and the saddle cloth was light-colored."

Rayth reined in his dun stallion and turned to look at me, brown eyes intent. "A triskelion?" he asked.

"If a triskelion is three spiral lines meeting to form a triangle at the center, then… yes?" I said.

"That mean something to you?" Eldris prodded, his attention focused on Rayth.

Rayth urged his horse into motion again, his face closing off. "It's the mark of Prince Oblisii. His personal crest."

Gladya made a noise of surprise. "Are you saying that one of these bandits worked for the prince?" she asked, sounding scandalized. "That doesn't make sense."

"Much more likely that the bandit stole a saddlecloth from someone under the prince's employ," Aristede said mildly. "Possibly also the horse it was attached to."

I looked back and forth between them. "Right. So, who's this Prince Oblisii, exactly?" I asked.

TWO

Rayth muttered something I couldn't make out. It didn't sound flattering.

Gladya trotted up to ride even with Aristede's horse. "He's the crown prince of Utrea, of course! King Khalafu's son. He wouldn't have anything to do with common bandits, I'm certain."

I thought about that for a bit.

"Even so," I said, "it seems like he'd want to know if someone wearing his crest was out attacking travelers in the desert. And he'd also want to know if his own men were being waylaid and their belongings stolen by bandits. I could petition the king…"

Rayth gave a quiet snort. I met his gaze with a hard look and raised an eyebrow at him.

"What?" I snapped. "You haven't exactly met me at my best, it's true—but I *do* happen to be the adopted daughter of one of the most powerful leaders on Eburos. Well… two of the most powerful leaders, I suppose. Have you heard of Senovo, the Wolf Priest of Draebard?"

"No," Rayth said. Gladya and Eldris echoed him with apologetic shrugs.

Aristede craned around to look at me over his shoulder, though. "The one who's supposed to be a shape-shifter?" he asked. "And who was mixed up in that Alyrion incursion back when I was a lad?"

He made a considering noise. "I always assumed that story was just an embellishment to make the Alyrion defeat sound a bit less humiliating than it actually was."

I looked at Aristede's sharply sculpted features in a new light. It was all too easy to be drawn in by his striking long hair with that odd white streak sweeping back from his forehead, and not notice the rest. But that patrician nose... those high cheekbones...

"Wait. Are you Alyrion?" I asked, feeling an odd twist of my stomach at the idea I might be riding with one of my people's longtime enemies.

I felt the muscles in his back stiffen for a moment before he seemed to consciously relax them.

"Me? I'm nobody in particular," he said in an easy, self-deprecating tone. "Though it is true I'm a nobody who was born on the western peninsula of Alyrios. I haven't lived there in many years. But do go on. You were speaking of your wolf priest?"

I took a breath and let it go. This was Utrea, not Alyrios. And, besides, while the Alyrions were responsible—indirectly, at least—for the death of my father and many other people I'd known as a girl, they'd maintained an uneasy peace with Eburos for more than a decade now. And the man seated in front of me was too young to have ever personally done anything to my home or loved ones.

"Senovo isn't a legend," I said, returning to the topic at hand. "He raised my brother and me after our parents died. So did the Draebardi chieftain who organized the defense against the Alyrion invasion."

"And your Horse Mistress, as well?" Gladya asked, looking at me curiously. "You were raised by three people?"

"Yes," I said, realizing I sounded a bit combative. I shook my head. "Look, it's kind of a long story. Suffice to say, I've got enough family connections to support a petition to the king, or at least to the prince. If nothing else, maybe I can get the authorities to go after these bandits, even if I can't track them down myself."

"Well," Gladya offered, "if there's anything I can do to help, I'll be happy to. I'm traveling to Safaad to meet my fiancé so we can finally get married. He's a distant nephew of the king's. I can ask him to put in a word for you, if you'd like."

I smiled at her, my earlier irritation fading. "Honestly, Gladya, I don't feel right asking you for anything else. You and your... uh—" I paused, not entirely sure what her connection was with the three men.

"Hired guards," Aristede supplied, sounding faintly amused.

"You and your guards have already done more than I can possibly repay," I finished.

Though I couldn't help being a bit jealous of Gladya's luck with choosing traveling companions compared to my own. Not only were the trio not backstabbing thieves—they were also quite a bit prettier to look at than either Omerah or Midhan had been.

And Rayth probably couldn't help being an aggravating sod. Maybe he'd had an unhappy upbringing or something, I thought charitably.

"Oh, come now," Gladya said, her full lips curving upwards, "we were hardly going to leave you lying insensible by the side of the road, now were we?"

"Believe me — my poor, sunburned breasts are eternally thankful for that fact," I told her, and felt Aristede's body move in silent laughter under my loose grip.

I relaxed against him, letting the mare's rolling gait lull my exhausted body as her hooves ate up the dusty road beneath us.

⚜

We rode until nearly dusk, when the path dipped into a valley dotted with the first plant life I'd seen since leaving Adumine and entering the uplands. I roused myself enough to look around.

"Is this the river Omerah talked about?" I asked, trying to peer into the lengthening shadows ahead of us.

Eldris snorted. "River? That's being generous."

The horses perked up, sniffing the air and increasing their pace without being urged. I tightened my grip on Aristede as his mare leapt into an easy canter, and he put a hand over my forearm to steady me.

"Snow melt from the mountains turns it into a reasonable watercourse during the spring," he said. "But I'm afraid at this time of year it's more of a runnel, when it's not completely dry. Still, the horses' reaction proves there's still water to be had for them."

My brief fantasy of a proper wash faded away as the animals descended the sandy bank, revealing darker earth at the bottom, broken only by the occasional puddle. Nonetheless, the horses enthusiastically waded into the shallow mud and started pawing at whatever tiny pool was nearest, widening and deepening the holes to reveal more muddy water as it seeped in. They drank thirstily, apparently unconcerned by its unappealing brown color.

"I suppose beggars can't be choosers," I offered. "I never really appreciated the importance of easy access to water before this."

"That's why the only people who live in the desert are nomads," Aristede said. "It's not so bad in the spring. Then, when it dries up, they simply pack their things and drive their goats elsewhere."

"I suppose that's why it was so hard to find people to travel with?" I asked. "Because it's summer?"

"Yeah, I expect so," said Eldris. "There's still a few caravans that run between the coast and the capital in late summer, but there are a lot more in the spring and early summer."

"It's also why I had to pay these three so much to come out and escort me to Safaad," Gladya said impishly.

Aristede lifted a hand to his chest as if she'd struck him with an arrow through the heart. "Ah, you wound us with your words, Lady Gladya.

With such fair company, this has surely been the most enjoyable coin we've ever earned."

I had already mentally labeled Aristede as a dangerous, silver-tongued temptation, and one to which I would happily have succumbed in other circumstances. But I was still bruised, sunburned, exhausted, and achy. Plus, I'd be camping in the open with other people tonight. Far better to enjoy that silver tongue in its linguistic capacity, and leave the rest alone. Not, I reflected, that he'd actually offered—or even implied—anything more. Though I judged it a remote chance, there was always the possibility that he was all talk and nothing else.

Besides, the look-but-don't-touch plan had the additional bonus of allowing me to covertly enjoy Eldris' unusual good looks as well. Hell, even Rayth was startlingly easy on the eyes as long as he kept his mouth shut. And, unlike Aristede, neither of those two struck me as the type to tumble strangers into bed on any kind of a regular basis. Certainly not Rayth, whose entire demeanor practically screamed *keep away, don't touch.*

Not that I had any interest in touching the irritating prick. *Obviously.*

Once the horses had refreshed themselves, the three men efficiently made camp. Gladya seemed content to leave them to it, and since she was paying, that seemed fair enough to me. I offered, but Eldris scowled and waved me off. Since I already had enough battles waiting to be fought, I shrugged easy agreement and flopped down next to the other woman.

"So. Tell me more about this man of yours," I said, eager to learn more about my rescuers. "Have you known him long?"

Gladya laughed, a clear and joyful sound. "Yes and no. We've only met three times, but we've been betrothed since he was ten and I was seven."

I blinked. "Hang on. You're marrying someone you've only met three times?"

Gladya looked at me curiously. "Well... yes. It's an exceptionally good match. I did mention that he's related to the royal house, didn't I? Of course, the part I didn't mention is that my family are merchants. Arranging the pairing was something of a coup for my mother. Darian's family gets a generous dowry, mine gets a guaranteed buyer for our spice trade, and I get a husband I'm honestly rather fond of. I'm even his first wife. Everybody wins."

I realized I was staring at her, and cleared my throat before blurting, "But you don't even know him! What if he's horrible?"

Even as the words came out, it occurred to me that they might not have been terribly diplomatic. Gladya tilted her head like a bird, but fortunately didn't appear offended.

"He's not horrible," she said. "Why would you think so? My parents would hardly have matched me with a brute. My older brother served in the cavalry with him for two years, and they became quite close friends. I found him quite charming company on the occasions when our parents brought us together. That's certainly basis enough for a good marriage."

I mulled over her words this time before speaking. "I think," I said slowly, "this might be another of those cultural things."

Her look of confusion cleared, and her mouth made an "Oh," shape.

The camp had taken shape around us as we spoke, and now Aristede sat down on the other side of the small fire Rayth had started with scrub wood.

"Hmm... I take it barbarian marriage customs are different?" he asked, softening what might have been an insult with a wickedly teasing smile.

"A bit, yeah," I replied dryly. "We don't have marriages, for one thing. We have handfastings. A priest binds the applicants' hands for a day and a night, and afterwards your lives are bound together unless you agree to go back to a priest and have the bonding severed. And while I won't deny that matchmaking is rampant among families within a village, handfastings generally end up being love matches."

Now I was on the receiving end of a shocked stare from Gladya. "Really? I... can't even picture how that would work. I mean, what if you fell in love with someone totally unsuitable?"

Aristede made a sound of amusement so faint I wasn't sure I'd actually heard it. I stifled a laugh of my own, though probably for different reasons. My three guardians back home were the very definition of an unsuitable match.

"If it comes down to it, you fight tooth and nail for love, unsuitable or not," I said. True, that might not have been the Eburosi way, as such—but it was what my brother Favian and I had grown up with. It was *our* way. "And if the gods are kind, you live happily ever after."

Eldris had joined us, handing a knife hilt-first to Aristede and tossing him some vegetables for chopping.

"Different customs, I guess," I offered. "For what it's worth, I can't really wrap my head around your way, either."

Eldris lifted an eyebrow. "If it makes you feel better, you might as well both be speaking a foreign language as far as I'm concerned. The Kulawi don't have marriage or handfasting or any of that shite. Two people wanna be together, they're together. They wanna be with someone else, they go be with someone else. The elders only step in if someone's sneaking around — not being honest and talking things out first. But as long as they are, who cares?"

"What about children, though?" I couldn't help asking, intrigued.

He stared back. "Eh? What about them? The village looks after its own, regardless of who's sleeping with whom or who fathered whom. Everyone's responsible for the children. They're the future."

"An eminently sensible approach, I've always thought," Aristede said, without looking up from his meal preparations.

I sat and thought about it, a slow smile crossing my lips at the picture Eldris had painted. "You know, this kind of thing is why I wanted to travel in the first place," I said. A laugh escaped me. "Well, this and the dragons."

Neither Aristede nor Eldris responded, and I wondered if I'd unintentionally put my foot in it somehow. An instant later, Gladya filled the sudden silence, though her smile was sad.

"I'm afraid there are no more dragons in Utrea," she said. "You're a few years too late for that."

"I know," I told her, sobering. "I learned that on the ocean voyage down from Eburos. But I'd still hoped to travel in the mountains... maybe see where they used to live." Even to see bones or broken eggshells from such magnificent creatures...

"The mountains are dangerous." It was the first contribution Rayth had made to the conversation since returning from caring for the horses.

"Oh?" I countered. "So is the trade road to Safaad, as it turns out. What's your point?"

Rayth ignored the question and took a deep draught from the waterskin he was holding.

"'Ere," Eldris said, reaching out one massive arm. "Hand that over for a minute. Might as well have wine instead of water in the stew."

So, not a waterskin, apparently. Eldris took the wine and poured some over the diced vegetables and strips of dried meat Aristede had added to the metal pot at his side. A few minutes later, the pot was bubbling merrily in the fast-burning fire.

"Tell me more about what happened to the dragons," I said, hugging my knees. "The man I talked to on the ship from Rhyth said that people killed them all, but he wouldn't go into detail."

Gladya mirrored me, her expression turning into a frown.

"It was King Khalafu's father," she said. "The Alyrion Empire was threatening Utrea's borders, but the Emperor feared the damage the dragonriders might do in the event of an all-out war. They say the old king was a little unstable—"

Rayth, who had been reunited with his wineskin as though it were a long-lost lover, made a derisive noise like a snort.

"—and he made a deal with the Alyrions," Gladya continued. "The Emperor offered him a peace treaty as long as he agreed to have all of the dragons in Utrea destroyed."

"You're joking," I said into the heavy silence that followed her words. "That's horrible!"

"Horrible and *stupid*," Gladya agreed, more passion in her voice than I had yet heard from her. After a moment, though, she looked down, her expression growing sheepish. "But don't tell anyone in Safaad I said that."

"You're right, though," I told her. "That was an awful decision! Destroy the one thing that was holding the Empire at bay? It's foolhardy."

Gladya shrugged, still looking down at her feet. "I suppose the king thought the peace treaty was more desirable than continuing tensions between the two countries. The Emperor gave him some trade concessions and other allowances, as well. So he sent the army out to kill all the adult dragons, and offered an outrageous bounty for anyone who brought him eggs."

"He decimated his bloody army while doin' it, too," Eldris muttered. "It's not like adult dragons are easy to kill."

"That wasn't the worst of it, though." Gladya's voice had gone so quiet that I had to strain to hear her words. "When the dragonriders protested, he had them imprisoned. Some of them were even executed... and the rest died soon afterward."

My heart gave an unhappy lurch. "The riders all died? Why? How?"

Gladya looked up at me, her brown eyes luminous in the firelight. "Their soul-bonds were broken when their dragons were killed."

I stared at her, trying to understand. "I don't know what that means."

She shook her head. "I'm not sure anyone who wasn't a dragonrider could really understand. But apparently, before a dragon accepted a rider, they had to form some kind of a connection. Mental... spiritual... I'm not really sure how it worked. But a wild dragon—an unbonded dragon—is nothing more than a dangerous beast. When dragons bonded with people, though, together they became something more. Something wonderful."

I swallowed, tears pricking at my eyes. "And when a bonded dragon died..." I began.

"Its rider died as well," she finished.

"Dear gods," I breathed, sickened at the callousness of what Utrea's king had done.

The others were silent. Rayth took another deep draught of the wine, and I idly wondered if it was unusual for him to spend his evenings pickling himself in spirits.

"Anyway," Gladya went on, "no one has seen an adult dragon in years, and the number of eggs turned in by the bounty hunters gradually dwindled to nothing. As far as anyone knows, they're all gone now."

"That may be one of the saddest things I've ever heard," I decided, imagining some poor, faceless soldier who'd served his king faithfully as a dragonrider, locked in a cell, feeling the animal he'd bonded to die... knowing he would soon follow.

"Stew's ready," Eldris mumbled, using a thick cloth wrapped around his hand to nudge the pot away from the fire. Maybe I was imagining it, but it seemed to me that his shoulders were taut with something. Anger, perhaps.

We ate, although I did so sparingly. Conversation was sporadic, none of us seeming much in the mood for stories or banter. Maybe I should have felt bad for dragging the mood down, but I'd wanted to know. Tales like this one were important. It was important that people remembered the awful things those in power did sometimes.

My childhood guardians had repelled an invasion by the very same empire that had threatened Utrea. My brother Favian and his two lovers had helped topple a corrupt king in the city-state of Rhyth. Meanwhile, I had merely stood to one side and watched these things happening around me — or heard about them, after the fact.

But if nothing else, I could tell this story so everyone would remember what had happened to the dragons in Utrea—and to the humans who'd loved them.

"You shouldn't go to the palace, Frella," Rayth said in a low voice, seemingly out of the blue.

He was still seated apart from the rest of us, and I'd noticed earlier that he'd refused the stew. The wineskin lying next to him was also considerably emptier than it had been the last time I'd paid attention. His words were not slurred, but they had that overly careful quality common to habitual drunkards. I narrowed my eyes, feeling my temper stir.

"While I appreciate your assistance in picking me up off the side of the road and helping me get to Safaad," I told him, "I don't really recall asking your opinion about what I should or shouldn't do once I arrive there."

He shrugged, not looking at me, something about the dismissive movement making me angrier. "Then you'll get my opinion for free," he replied. "If you're smart, you'll turn around and head straight back north to your barbarian island. Go home to your powerful guardians, and don't risk yourself in pursuit of whatever it is you've traveled across the sea to find."

I stood up slowly, facing him, snapping my jaw shut when I realized that it was hanging open in outrage. "How dare you?" I asked, genuinely taken aback at his casual dismissal of the ambition for travel I'd harbored for as long as I could remember.

"Utrea can be a dangerous place," he muttered, still staring into the crackling flames rather than looking at me.

"I can take care of myself!" I snapped.

At that, he finally met my eyes and lifted one arched brow. "Can you indeed?" he asked in that dry-as-dust drawl I was quickly coming to hate.

I felt my sun-reddened cheeks heat yet again as I contemplated my current position, wearing borrowed clothes and eating other peoples' food as I prepared to spend another day begging a ride on someone else's horse. Possibly, the reasonable thing to do at that point would have been to sit my ass down and shut my mouth.

So, of course, what I actually did was stomp over to where Rayth was lounging against his saddle and jab a finger at his face. "Why don't you come over here and I'll show you just how well I can take care of myself... assuming you can part with your wineskin long enough for a sparring match."

Why... *why* did I do things like this? My preferred weapons were crossbow, quarterstaff, and throwing knives. Weapons designed to keep larger and stronger opponents from getting close enough to make use of their advantages over me. And right now, I had precisely none of those things available. When I discovered that I wouldn't be able to find the right kind of crossbow bolts in Utrea, I'd bartered my bow as part of the payment for Laduna. A staff was impractical to stow for long-distance travel on horseback, and my throwing knives were now the property of the bastards who'd waylaid me earlier today.

At least Rayth was drunk off his ass. That would probably be enough of a disadvantage for me to be able to take him.

Across the fire from us, Eldris made an interested noise. "A sparring match? This I gotta see."

"Don't be ridiculous," Rayth said dismissively, still in that precisely enunciated voice.

A low whistle caught my attention, and when I turned, Aristede tossed me a dagger nestled in a leather sheath, hilt-first. "You'll be wanting this," he said. "Try not to skewer him for real. That could be awkward."

"Do you good to get a little sparring in, Rayth," Eldris opined, leaning back and lacing his fingers together behind his head, the hard muscles in his chest flexing as he did.

When I turned back, Rayth had risen silently, and we were suddenly standing much too close. I took a step back, and then mentally cursed myself for having yielded ground. He was... very tall. How had I not noticed that before?

"Are you both quite sure about this?" Gladya asked, sounding anything but.

"Oh, yeah. Totally," I lied, putting more space between us since I'd already taken that first telling step. He was drunk, I reminded myself. Completely shit-faced. It would be fine.

I shook out my bruised and aching limbs as best I could, checking the area around us to make sure we wouldn't accidentally damage something important. "So, daggers then?" I asked, trying to get a feel for Rayth's style as he moved toward me.

"Dagger. Singular," he said. His bloodshot eyes flicked to the knife in my hand. "That one."

All righty, then. He was apparently going to spar unarmed out of some ridiculous notion of chivalry. Great. This was totally doable.

"It's your funeral," I told him. A snort, quickly stifled, came from one of the others behind me.

I was trying to decide whether to play defense or offense when Rayth lunged, taking the decision from me. I sidestepped, only to find that it had been a feint and he was still directly in my path. I brought the blade up, flat side out since we were sparring, and he caught my wrist. With a violent twist, I wrenched free and whirled away, coming to a stop a couple strides away from him.

Damn it… he was moving far too fast and with far too much precision for someone who had single-handedly drained half of a wineskin over the course of an hour.

In my defense, if the knife Aristede gave me had been weighted for throwing—which it wasn't—I could have had it lodged in Rayth's throat in an instant as we stood across from each other. But skewering was definitely off the table tonight, even if Rayth *was* an annoying prick. I'd have to do this the hard way, unless I wanted to back down like a coward.

I didn't want to back down. I wanted to put Rayth's drunken ass on the ground to prove a point about… something.

I feinted left and used the moment as Rayth reacted to tangle my leg with both of his. Momentum allowed me to drive an elbow into his back as our bodies twisted around each other, and he went down. In fact, he went down far more easily than I had expected. The reason for this became apparent when his knees tightened around the leg I'd tangled between his and jerked me sideways, pulling me down after him.

A good-natured catcall came from the small audience. I thought it was probably Eldris, but couldn't really spare time to focus on it. The good news was, I'd landed on top of Rayth, and my knife arm was still free. Normally, I would have gone for a knee to the groin, but the way he was keeping our legs tangled together made me think he was expecting that.

I twisted my upper body, attempting to get the point of the knife aimed at his ribs, which would effectively end the fight. A lean, corded arm wound around mine, his superior strength ensuring I couldn't get the blade turned toward his body. Hoping that he would discount my left hand, I threw my weight against our tangled arms despite the way it twisted my elbow.

My left fist flew out, trying for the same neck jab I'd attempted against Eldris on the road earlier. I'd intended to pull the punch, obviously, but Rayth jerked his chin down to protect his throat and my knuckles hit his jaw instead, with more force than I had intended.

He grunted, but didn't loosen his hold on me. An instant later, the world shifted around me and I was somehow pinned on my back, breathing hard, the hilt of the dagger no longer in my hand and both of my wrists above my head in an unbreakable grip. Hard brown eyes, glittering in the firelight, stared down at me from a scruffy, high-cheekboned face.

"And that," he said, his breath smelling of the wine he'd consumed, "was against an unarmed drunkard."

THREE

Fury—fueled at least partly by embarrassment and partly by my sudden, visceral awareness of his body pressed against mine—made me buck and squirm beneath him.

"I'm better with ranged weapons," I hissed through gritted teeth, and wriggled again.

My pelvis rolled against his. It was completely unintentional on my part, but I felt a noticeable twitch of hard flesh against the crease of my thigh in the instant before he pushed away from me and stood up. I eyed the hand he extended to me for a long moment before taking it with bad grace and allowing him to pull me to my feet. His expression was once more cold and distant.

"Well fought," Aristede said, clapping in a way that did not seem to be mocking.

Still, I had to hold back the torrent of arguments and excuses that wanted to fly to my lips—it *hadn't* been well fought, but if I weren't tired and sore I would have done better. If I'd had my preferred weapons, I wouldn't have ended up on my back with Rayth's prick poking me in the hip. If he'd had the good grace to fight like someone who'd drunk enough wine to swim in… if he hadn't riled me up first by being such a conceited ass…

Excuses have never won a single fight, Kitten. I could practically hear Ithric's words in my ear, even though he was half a world away. *And while having a vicious temper may have won a few, it's responsible for losing many more. Go on — ask me how I know.*

I deflated.

"Not that well fought," I told Aristede. Steeling myself, I glanced at Rayth and choked back my pride. "Look, I take your point. But just because travel is dangerous doesn't mean I'm not going to do it anyway. It's my life. Mine to risk; mine to control."

He cocked an eyebrow. "Yours to lose, if you choose to risk it on the wrong thing at the wrong time."

"Yes," I agreed, not willing to fight anymore tonight. "That, too."

"Don't discount yourself," Aristede said. "Rayth is a trained soldier, and you made him work for it despite being exhausted and battered. You've got talent, even if melee fighting isn't your preferred style."

Honestly, it hadn't seemed from my perspective like he'd had to work all *that* hard, but Eldris nodded agreement.

"I could show you a few things," said the big man. Then, he seemed to catch himself. "But you're too tired tonight… and I guess there won't be much chance once we get to Safaad tomorrow."

I felt an unexpected tinge of regret upon realizing he was right.

"Yeah, I guess not," I said. "Still—thanks for offering. I'd take you up on it if I could."

The corner of his lush lips twitched in a roguish half-smile. "Eh, don't mind me. I'm just jealous 'cause I didn't get to roll around in the dirt with you."

I choked on a very unladylike snort of laughter, even as the tingly feeling which had made an unwanted appearance in my belly when Rayth had gained the upper hand on me returned. Thankfully, I was saved from having to come up with a witty response by Gladya's quiet voice.

"I admire your bravery," she said. "I'd love to visit faraway lands, but the idea of actually doing so terrifies me. Learning a whole new language? Different customs? Not knowing any of the people or places? I couldn't do it."

I shook my head. "I'm not brave, Gladya. Just stubborn. If you want to travel, you should travel. You don't have to sail for the farthest horizon like me. You could visit somewhere closer. I mean... come on." I gestured at the camp around us. "You're traveling *now*."

She looked up, her large brown eyes meeting mine. A little smile tugged at her full lips. "Well, I suppose you're right. Who knows? Perhaps I will, someday, with Darian."

"That's a fair point about the language," Eldris mused, leaning back on his elbows to regard me. "Where'd you learn to speak Utrean so well, anyway?"

I shrugged. "No mystery there. An Utrean scholar came to Rhyth to consult with one of the priests from my home village. An old guy by the name of Ghizaan. He's the one who convinced me to come to Utrea, though I suspect that some of his stories were more than a little embellished." I sobered. "The ones about dragons certainly were. But, anyway, he taught me the language. He stayed for more than a year, and I think he enjoyed having someone to talk to in his native tongue."

He nodded, and I collapsed back into my place near the fire.

"What about you?" I asked, curious. "How did you learn it?"

Eldris shifted. "Picked it up in the army, didn't I?" he said. "Things at home got a bit messy, so I traveled up the coast to see if I could find better prospects elsewhere. I taught myself a few phrases along the way, but the military commanders only cared that I could pummel their best fighters and look scary while wielding an axe. They weren't too fussed about my oration skills."

I suspected there was a lot more to his story than I was going to be able to get in the short time I had available, and a part of me regretted that. Now, though, Rayth stirred.

"We should get some rest," he said. "I'll take the first watch."

I wondered if anyone else in the group would object to that, knowing how much wine he'd put away, but no one did. I noted with interest, though, the casual way in which Aristede wandered over and helped himself to a drink from what was left in the skin, then somehow neglected to return it to Rayth afterward.

"I can take a watch," I offered, but Gladya only laughed.

"Nonsense, my dear. First, you must be about to collapse after the day you've had, and second, I'm paying good money for these fine men to take care of me."

I chuckled, giving in without argument. "All right, then. I *am* pretty tired, so… offer withdrawn, in that case."

"As it should be," Aristede said, mock severe. He turned to Eldris. "You want the second watch, my friend?"

"Sure, I'm easy," Eldris agreed. "I'll wake you up for the last one, or if…" He trailed off for a moment. "… you know."

Aristede's smile had a tight quality to it. "Quite," he said. "Good night, all."

Rayth grunted, and the rest of us echoed Aristede's sentiment.

I settled down close to the sputtering scrub-wood fire and wrapped my borrowed blanket around my body. Despite my aches and bruises, it felt like only moments until I drifted off.

⤟ ⚜ ⤝

I awoke only once, to the sound of a scuffle and a low cry. I thought for a moment that it had just been a dream, but Eldris' low voice followed after a short pause.

"Easy. You all right now, Ari?" he asked, the words barely a whisper.

There was a longer pause, and then a groggy voice, "I… yes. I'm fine. Is it time for my watch?"

"Not really."

The fire had gone out, only starlight illuminating the riverbed around us. I heard the rustling of a blanket being tossed off. "Never mind. I'm up; you might as well get some sleep."

"If you're sure."

"I'm sure."

More rustling, and then silence settled over the camp, broken only by the tiny night sounds of insects and other small desert creatures. Before long, sleep claimed me again. The next time my eyes opened, it was light.

"Time to get up," Gladya said.

I made an incoherent noise and she smiled down at me, patting the shoulder she'd shaken to wake me. Somehow, she still managed to look cool and elegant despite her messy hair. By contrast, I suspected that I resembled a sun-reddened troll, with puffy eyes, rumpled clothing, and rats' nests tangled amongst my honey-colored locks.

"Ugh," I managed, language still beyond me.

A steaming cup appeared in my line of sight. I looked up in time to see Aristede throw me a mischievous wink, though I couldn't help noticing the pale cast to his golden skin and the dark smudges under his eyes.

"Thanks," I rasped, rolling into a sitting position and discovering an entirely new set of aches from the previous day's adventures.

The cup contained spicy tea, and did an admirable job of kicking my groggy wits into full wakefulness.

"This is good," I said, as Eldris walked by and handed me a round of flatbread. "What is it?"

"Valdarium root with rignan flower," Aristede called. He was already gathering up the supplies and packing them.

I looked around, and realized that the saddles were gone—Rayth must have gone to tack up the horses. It was clear we wouldn't be dallying, so as soon as I was done eating and drinking, I forced protesting muscles into use and rose to my feet. There wasn't much in the way of cover, but I found a pile of rocks a short way along the riverbed and went behind them to relieve myself.

After quickly dragging my hands through my thick hair to loosen the worst of the tangles, I pulled three hanks back from my forehead and temples, quickly plaiting them to keep hair out of my face. By the time I was ready, so was everyone else. I put aside my niggle of guilt at not having been more of a help with packing up the camp, figuring that probably fell under the auspices of what the three men were being paid for.

I swung up behind Aristede again, wincing a bit as my body protested the exertion. The horses had a final drink, and we headed off without ceremony. Conversation was sporadic, and I made little effort to add to it, choosing instead to doze against Aristede's broad back. It was not a half-bad place to be, all things considered—though it did grow hot as the unforgiving sun rose overhead.

When the bay mare's head began to droop as the sun passed its zenith, Rayth decreed that I would ride the rest of the way with him. I couldn't very well protest. Eldris was a massive man, and though his horse was strongly built, he was already carrying more weight than the others. Gladya was slender and light, but her gray was a short, delicate thing.

So I rode with Rayth, and tried not to resent the fact that he helped me vault up with the same effortless strength and timing that Aristede had shown, *or* the fact that I was painfully aware of every single place where my body pressed against his.

Needless to say, I didn't doze any more.

It wasn't quite accurate to say that Rayth seemed none the worse for wear after his heavy indulgence the previous evening. He'd been surly and taciturn that morning, and gave the sun the same disdainful regard one might give a manure stain on one's tunic. Nevertheless, his back was straight in the saddle and his hand steady on the reins. His head tilted this way and that as he scanned the horizon for danger.

A habitual drunkard, then, I was sure. His body had become accustomed to regular overindulgence, to the point that spirits no longer affected him as they would most people. Such a lifestyle came with costs, I knew, and generally stemmed from an unhappy past left to fester.

But that was no business of mine.

As the sun sank toward the horizon and the desert gave way to fertile front-range, the city of Safaad came into view. It was built into the base of the mountains, spires and towers rising from the rock. Despite my aches and bruises, I couldn't help the smile that pulled at my chapped lips.

It was beautiful. Exotic. Different than any city I had seen before. I adored it immediately.

As we closed the final few leagues, I realized it was also much larger and more sprawling than it appeared from a distance. Some of those towers were truly a staggering height, putting to shame even the tallest buildings in Rhyth. The roads were paved in cobblestone, growing steep and winding as we entered the city. The horses' hooves clattered over them, echoing against the stone walls on either side.

The smaller, less ornate buildings on the outskirts appeared to be private homes and merchants' storefronts. As we traveled uphill, going deeper into the city, the buildings grew more impressive. It was hard to keep my bearings—the streets appeared to follow the natural contours of the mountains into which they'd been built, rather than any sort of grid or other logical layout. There were switchbacks and blind corners, dead ends and loops, all bustling with a surprising amount of traffic as evening shadows swallowed the light.

Lamplighters emerged, using long poles to ignite the oil lamps hanging high on the walls of buildings, illuminating the streets in a mellow, flickering glow as the last light faded. Eventually, we arrived at a grand wall surrounding buildings that shone with colored tiles and beaten metal domes. I took this to be the palace complex—confirmed a few moments later when our little party drew to a halt.

Gladya looked up at the massive gates with glowing eyes, obviously excited to have arrived at her destination. She turned to me, a smile curving her delicate lips.

"Darian is to meet me in the guest wing of the palace this evening," she said. "We will not be staying there, however—he has his own residence a little distance from here. If you need somewhere to stay tonight—"

I slid down from Rayth's stallion and cut her off. "Gladya, I can't accept anything more from you. You've already been too kind, and I'm not about to impose on you and Darian now that you're finally together."

I worked my fingers into the thick hair falling over my neck, locating one of the lengths of delicate gold chain braided into the locks underneath and picking it loose. A few strands of hair snapped, still tangled in the chain. I winced a bit at the sting as I pulled out the hidden gemstone, set in a fine metal clasp and hanging from the bottom link.

"In fact," I continued, "I want to repay you for your generosity, if you'll allow it." I couldn't help the way my gaze flickered up to Rayth's for an instant, or the dry tone that entered my voice. "As you see, I haven't been left completely without resources."

Gladya laughed, delighted. "Oh, my dear!" she said. "You *are* full of surprises! But, no, I cannot accept payment for common courtesy. Your company was most welcome, and I'm only pleased that my guards and I were able to help. If you're certain you won't stay as my guest tonight, then you should be able to find a moneychanger still open, if you're quick. Exchange your hidden gem for enough coin to replace your lost clothing and supplies, and rent a room somewhere safe. I do wish you'd allow me to ease your way in for a meeting with the prince, though."

I smiled back. "I don't think that will be necessary. I'll arrange something tomorrow, once I've acquired some new clothes and gotten a night's rest in an actual bed." I nestled the gem in the pocket of my breeches, and walked over to Gladya's horse. "Now, go on. Your man is waiting for you and I've already delayed your reunion more than enough."

Gladya's grin grew even more brilliant. She leaned down and I stretched up enough to exchange a quick embrace. "It was a pleasure to meet you, Frella of Draebard. I'm honored to have made the acquaintance of an Eburosi barbarian."

It was my turn to laugh. "Try not to hold me against the rest of my clansmen," I told her and turned to the men. "Thank you. I only wish I'd come upon the four of you in Adumine, rather than ending up with Omerah and Midhan."

Eldris grinned, and Aristede's mouth quirked at the corner. Rayth, to no great surprise, remained expressionless.

"For what it's worth," Aristede offered, "Eldris and I will be staying at the Purple Cloak for a few days, should you have need of anything."

Argh. *There* was a temptation I really didn't need. Again, the offer might have been completely innocent… or it might not have been. I couldn't deny the appeal of taking Eldris up on his earlier offer of teaching me some new defensive moves. Or of seeing if Aristede was interested in a quick tumble in bed.

Perhaps I would give into that temptation once I'd spoken to the King or the Prince. What harm would there be? Especially if Rayth was engaged elsewhere, as Aristede had seemed to imply.

"I'll keep that in mind," I said, not wanting to commit to anything, but also wanting to keep that door open. "Now, though, could someone point me to the nearest moneychanger?"

Half an hour later, I strolled out of a neat two-story building with a new coin purse hanging at my waist, its weight a comfort as I looked around and headed for the nearest building that looked like it offered rooms. It was growing late, I was exhausted, and I decided to wait until morning to take care of the rest of my purchases. An extra coin brought me a bowl of spicy stew and a carafe of watered wine.

Stomach sated, I fell asleep on the comfortable mattress and slept like the dead. And if I dreamed of ebony skin or eyes the color of forged steel? Well, my dreams were my own, and there was no one around to comment on the matter.

FOUR

The next morning was a whirlwind of shopping and sightseeing. Safaad truly was a wonder. Even in Rhyth, I had never seen such stunning architecture. I could scarcely imagine how people could have lifted heavy stone and metal to the great heights necessary to complete the towers that capped the palace.

In addition, everything was bursting with color—vibrant reds, blues, oranges, and greens vied to draw the eye, each building more vibrant than the last. Despite the difficult journey from the nearest port town, the shops and tents in the market district offered every delight one could possibly want.

It was a different sort of prosperity than I was used to. In northern Eburos, food and basic necessities were generally plentiful. The forests and fields teemed with game and edible plants. Villagers often raised plots of vegetables and grains, or kept cattle, pigs, goats, and chickens for meat and eggs. Clothing was fashioned from leather and hide, or woven from natural fiber. We mined gold, silver, copper, tin, iron, and precious stones. The lush forests provided lumber and fuel.

In Rhyth, where my brother lived, corruption and civil war had decimated the economy, which was based more on trade than subsistence. In the decade since the people had risen up and expelled the despotic king, things had improved. However, Rhyth still struggled to ensure that all its citizens had access to the basic necessities. The city had its luxuries, like the extravagant bathhouses, but exotic, high-end goods were often hard to come by.

Safaad appeared to have no such problem, and I wondered if the place held hidden pockets of poverty, or if it really was as prosperous as it seemed. I couldn't deny the pleasure I took from browsing through stall after stall of beautiful fabrics and clothing, looking for the perfect items to replace what had been stolen from me. I knew I had to be smart about things — while it was true I was carrying a small fortune braided into my heavy length of hair, I had no easy way to earn more money once the gems were gone.

So, I made myself stay practical for the most part, though I did purchase one rather extravagant outfit. I justified it as a necessity for being taken seriously at the palace. If I was going to play on my connection to foreign political power, I needed to look the part.

After spending an enjoyable hour going through the weapon-makers' wares, I settled on a set of six throwing knives — not wanting to be caught in the same situation I had been on the road. Of course, the irony was, they would do me no good whatsoever today. If the palace guards allowed me entrance with so much as a knitting needle on my person, I'd be shocked.

Still, I'd just spent a morning wandering around the city without seeing a single thing to make me think the place was dangerous. Women bustled around with no sign of fear, their children playing in the squares and courtyards. Armed men I took to be city guards were a regular presence, but the city folk did not cringe from them or evince worry at their presence. I'd even seen people stop and chat with them.

All in all, the place gave every indication of being a safe, flourishing center of art and commerce. And why not? They were at peace with their powerful neighbors, enjoying lucrative treaties and trade deals with a sprawling empire.

And all it had taken was the eradication of an entire population of amazing, irreplaceable animals, along with the humans who had loved them.

With that knowledge in mind, the glitter and shine of the place seemed noticeably duller. I disagreed passionately with the king who had made that choice and sentenced all those lives to execution, but I also didn't know what it felt like to hold the responsibility for a kingdom full of people.

I'd been raised by people who would rather fight and die than face enslavement. That had informed my outlook on life, I knew. How could it not? But I could still understand how a ruler might look at the children frolicking around the market square and see the horrible things that could happen to them during a war.

In some ways, I had been groomed for leadership. Though adopted, I was still the child of Andoc, a powerful village chieftain. With my brother occupied in Rhyth, I was the *only* child who might conceivably wish to step into his role someday. I didn't want it, though. There were others better suited, and as far as I was concerned, they were welcome to it. Let one of Jacun and Varanis' children take over when the time came. That would solidify our treaty with our allies in Meren, which was far more important than keeping the chieftainship in the family, so to speak.

They'd probably do a better job, anyway. Having a fiery temper and a tendency toward wanderlust didn't really make for a good leader.

I stood before the oval-shaped metal mirror in my rented room, arranging the draped material of the dress I'd just purchased in such a way as to accentuate my curves as elegantly as possible. Gods, it was a beautiful confection of a thing—filmy in all the right places, and a beautiful shade of light blue, bringing out my eyes. It felt a bit odd not to be dressed for travel, but even a northern barbarian knew better than to show up for an audience with royalty dressed in stained breeches and a plain linen tunic.

I pulled on soft slippers and wiggled my toes a bit. We didn't really have anything like these back home—you either wore boots, sandals, or went barefoot. They were pretty, though. Dyed the same color as the dress, and so light that it wasn't much different than going barefoot. I decided that I liked them.

The palace gate where I'd said goodbye to the others was only a few minutes' walk from my room. I'd left my knife-belt behind, trusting my instincts that the central part of the city was safe during broad daylight. Indeed, no one molested me, though a few did stare — possibly drawn either to the dress, my unusual hair and eye color, or both. I only smiled back, and waggled my fingers in a little wave at the young boy who tugged on his mother's hand and pointed at me with wide, dark eyes.

The gates were every bit as impressive in daylight as they had been last night. Half a dozen guards stood impassively, three on either side.

"Hello," I said to the one who looked oldest and like he might be in charge. "I'm the daughter of a foreign dignitary, and I was hoping you could tell me who I might speak to about arranging an audience."

See? I could be diplomatic.

The guard's eyes swept over me appraisingly, his gaze thorough and professional. "The king holds audiences three times a week. As it happens, there will be one today, beginning when the sun touches the top of the west wall. You will need to speak to his majesty's vizier to arrange it. This guard will take you to him."

That was easy, I thought.

"Thank you," I told him, as he gestured to a much younger guard, who stepped forward and dipped his head to me respectfully.

I followed him into the palace complex, which was shady and cool compared to the streets baking in the sun outside. Nestled at the base of the mountains, Safaad was not nearly as hot as the unforgiving desert, but it was still a warm and arid place. The sound of water trickling in stone fountains was welcome inside the rich surroundings.

The vizier was a gray-haired old man with gaunt features and a vaguely harried demeanor. He asked me a few questions before dipping a sharpened stick into a pot of ink and making a series of squiggles on a piece of parchment. I recognized them as the Utrean version of the written symbols used by some people in Alyrios and Rhyth. My old friend Ghizaan had tried to show them to me, back when he was teaching me the language.

Unfortunately, while I apparently had a good head for learning new tongues, it was not nearly so good with written languages. I had a basic grasp of Rhytherii symbols after much practice, but Utrean still looked to me like someone had dunked a bunch of caterpillars in ink and let them crawl randomly across the parchment. Ghizaan had eventually given up on me, at least in that regard.

Once I had answered the vizier's questions, I was chivvied away to a waiting area where several other people were loitering, clearly awaiting their turn for an audience, as I was. I found the wide variation in their apparent wealth and social standing surprising, but in a good way. It seemed that the royal family was at least open to hearing petitions from those who were not themselves powerful, which was more than the former king of Rhyth could have said, certainly.

I considered trying to strike up a conversation, but my companions appeared largely wrapped up in their own thoughts. I supposed one only came to petition the king when there was a problem to be addressed. Certainly, I was only here because of the attack I'd suffered on the trade road.

Not wanting to impose, I found an unoccupied seat and kept my mouth shut. A few minutes later, a new arrival entered the waiting area. He was an older man, with gray peppering his dark hair, and wrinkles in his sun-lined face. He cast a glance around the place and his eyes settled on me. A friendly smile crossed his face, and he gestured at the seat next to mine.

"May I?" he asked in a pleasant voice.

I swept a hand out in invitation, returning his smile. "Be my guest. I'm Frella."

"Vitraal," he replied. "Nice to meet you. Not a local, I take it?"

"Ooh, does it show?" I teased, and he laughed softly. "No, I'm from Eburos. I'm traveling the continent, and I was attacked by bandits on the trade road from Adumine. One of the men had a saddle blanket bearing the crest of Prince Oblisii, so I thought he might want to know about it."

Vitraal's face darkened momentarily, before he consciously smoothed his expression. "That's unfortunate," he said. "I hope you weren't injured during the attack?"

I shrugged. "Scrapes and bruises, plus an unfortunate case of sunburn from being stuck in the desert until someone happened by and rescued me. The gang stole my horse and most of my possessions, though."

56

"Not a very appealing introduction to our land, I fear," Vitraal said mildly. "Still, you've chosen an advantageous day to visit the palace. The king will be hearing petitions personally this afternoon."

I nodded. "Really? I wasn't sure how that worked. Honestly, I'd figured it would be just as good if I spoke directly with the prince, since it was his crest I saw on the bandit's saddle cloth."

Vitraal tried to smile, but the expression appeared tight. "It's for the best if you speak to King Khalafu instead, since you have the chance. The prince is…"

He trailed off, and I raised my eyebrows. "The prince is…?" I prompted.

But he only shook his head. "Ah — don't mind me. It's nothing. Just tell the king what happened, and I'm sure he'll do whatever he can. Yours is certainly a far more compelling tale than my own on this fine day."

"Oh?" I asked. "And what is your tale?"

His smile this time looked more genuine. "Tiresome matters of business, I fear. I am a spokesman for the weavers' guild, and the dye merchants have recently doubled their prices with no real explanation. I've been sent to request that the prices for indigo be capped until the next harvest of blue knotweed arrives in a few months. Fascinating stuff, I know."

I chuckled. "Trade is important," I told him. "I expect your petition will affect a lot more people than mine will."

He shook his head. "Nonsense. Bandits on the trade road? It might be the off season for travel, but that's serious." He glanced across the room as an official-looking man beckoned the first of the waiting people through an interior archway. "It looks like they're getting underway. So, tell me — what brings you to Utrea in the first place? And from such a far-flung land…"

Vitraal and I passed a pleasant stretch chatting about my travels and the city in which I now found myself. Whenever the topic strayed too near politics, I noticed that he grew tense and guided it away again. It made me curious, but I had no wish to make the man uncomfortable, so I didn't push.

Eventually, the official at the door indicated me with a raised finger, and gestured for me to follow. I gave Vitraal a final smile, along with a word of farewell. My surroundings seemed to grow even more luxurious as we traveled deeper into the palace, and I got the distinct impression the route was intended to instill awe in the petitioners during the moments before they were presented to the king. It was, I had to admit, fairly effective.

The great, echoing hallways were inlaid with tiles of gold and vivid red. Rather than the pillars and flat ceilings I was used to back home, the supports arched to meet at the top of dome-like vaults far above my head, each one identical to the last. Eventually, the hallway opened into a large space dominated by a dais at the far end, with a simple throne at the center. Stone steps led up to the raised platform where several people awaited. The entire room was hung with intricate tapestries covering the walls—some with complex geometric patterns, and others depicting human and animal figures.

All this hit me in the space of a few heartbeats as I glanced around, standing just outside the open double doors. The palace official gestured me to go through, and my eyes fell on the vizier I'd spoken with earlier, standing a few paces inside. He cleared his throat and spoke in a resonant voice that would carry to the throne and the figure seated on it.

"Your Majesty, I present to you Frella of Draebard, daughter of High Chieftain Andoc of Draebard, from the Isle of Eburos," he intoned. "Here to offer a report of banditry on the trade road from Adumine!"

At a flick of the vizier's eyes toward the throne, I walked forward, trying to get a sense of the Utrean ruler without blatantly staring at him. My first impression was of advanced age, though a second glance showed that his hair was not yet completely gray. His face, however, was wrinkled and sunken, as if from some sort of wasting disease.

A handful of other men stood behind the throne, one positioned closer to the king than the others. He was a sharp-faced man, richly dressed. Handsome, but with a cast of cruelty marring his features. Thick brown hair fell back from his face in waves, and his dark eyes caught mine as I tried to study him surreptitiously, making blood rush to my cheeks as I quickly looked away.

The stone steps leading up to the dais were narrow, and two impassive guards stood at the bottom in silent menace, armed with blades mounted on the ends of staves. Their skin was almost as dark as Eldris' had been, but their faces held none of his innate good cheer.

I stopped a few steps back from them and dipped to one knee, unsure of the correct protocol. I'd always hated this kind of stupid bowing and scraping, but I also knew it was generally better to overdo things a bit than to come across as too arrogant.

After a moment's contemplation, the king said, "Daughter of a barbarian chieftain, eh? Where is your retinue, child?"

His voice had that slightly hoarse quality that the elderly often exhibited, but his words and demeanor were pleasant enough. I straightened my bowed head, but didn't rise from my half-kneeling position as I replied.

"I am not here as an envoy, Your Majesty. Merely as a traveler. I have no retinue."

It was the cruel-eyed man standing next to the throne who answered. "No retinue? So you were traveling alone—a woman, no less—when you were set upon by bandits?"

It was so close to the words Rayth had thrown at me two days ago that I inwardly bristled. No doubt there was a reason this man was standing in such a favored position next to the king, however. For that reason, I swallowed my irritation before responding.

"I was not traveling alone," I said, already tired of the story after only a couple of retellings. "The caravan I was slated to join cancelled when the ship carrying their cargo failed to dock, and I was forced to seek out other guides to get me to Safaad. Unfortunately, the couple I found apparently makes their livelihood by luring unsuspecting travelers into an ambush in the middle of the desert. After which, they abscond with their victim's valuables and leave them to rot."

"A shocking occurrence," the king said, his brows twitching together above his rheumy eyes. "And not the sort of welcome Utrea desires to offer travelers to its shores."

"I'm sure my money and belongings are long gone," I began, "but they also stole my horse, and—"

"I will ensure that additional patrols are deployed along the trade road, my dear," said the king, cutting across my words. "Rest assured that these bandits will be caught and punished."

I swallowed a sigh. *Yeah, sure they will.* I recognized a polite brush-off when I heard one. Still, I wasn't quite ready to let it go.

"The couple's names were Omerah and Midhan. There were four bandits in the gang that descended on us, and one of them had the mark of Prince Oblisii on his saddle cloth—a triskelion, I believe it's called."

King Khalafu's bushy eyebrows lifted, and he shot a glance over his shoulder. "Indeed?" he asked in his reedy voice, as the younger man next to him stiffened slightly. "Well, young woman… perhaps I will leave you in my son's hands. Obviously, I have no knowledge about any such thing."

With a faint jolt, I realized that the man who had spent the past few minutes undressing me with his flat, dark gaze must be the prince in question. And his presence was about as reassuring as a coiled snake's. Terrific.

Now, the question was, how far would I allow my own stubbornness to push the matter? My better sense was telling me to bow and scrape a couple more times, and then hightail it out of the palace as fast as my feet would carry me. Perhaps to scamper straight to the Purple Cloak and throw myself on Aristede's and Eldris' hospitality for the night… or longer.

My pride, on the other hand, was telling me that running like a spooked rabbit wouldn't get Laduna back. This man was a prince, for the gods' sake — and I was a chieftain's daughter, albeit an adopted one. What did I think he was going to do to me? I shook off my odd frisson of unease.

"You're Prince Oblisii, then?" I asked, just to be sure.

One sharp eyebrow arched. "I am indeed." His eyes did that thing again, raking over my body as though he could see right through the draped fabric of the dress. Though, to be fair, it *was* kind of filmy in places — albeit tastefully so.

I cleared my throat, hoping to draw his attention back to my face. "So, do you think the bandits stole that saddlecloth from one of your men?" I asked. "Have any of your guards reported items missing lately?"

A look of boredom flitted across the prince's face. "I will look into things as soon as time permits," he said carelessly. "In the mean time, please allow me to extend you the hospitality of the palace. Consider yourself my personal guest."

Part of me still wanted to make a run for the Purple Cloak, but that was foolish. There was no point in turning down free accommodations, especially when leaving would mean I needed to go through the entire process of meeting with the vizier and waiting around for access to the throne room again. I was being silly.

I pasted a smile on my face and dipped my head again. "Thank you. I'm sure everything can be sorted out easily enough. Perhaps someone could get me a list of the places where someone might go to sell a horse with no questions—

Again, I was cut off.

"Yes, yes," the prince said, waving one hand imperiously. A figure I hadn't noticed detached herself from the wall and approached me, head bowed. "Go with this girl. She will take you to your accommodations. Girl, take my guest to the western quarters."

I rose to my feet, my muscles protesting a bit after the exertions of the past few days. "Uh... all right, then. Thank you again for speaking with me..."

For all the good it seems to have done, I didn't add.

"Come with me, please," said the girl, in a low voice.

She was pretty, in a plain sort of way. A few years younger than I was, I guessed, and a tiny bit shorter—which was saying something. I let her lead me out of a side entrance in the throne room, and only spoke when the heavy door shut behind us.

"Hello, there," I said trying and failing to catch her eye as she bustled forward, her head still bent. "I'm Frella. What's your name?"

"Beshaam," she replied, halfway between a whisper and a squeak.

I wondered what I'd done to spook her... or what someone else had done. "Nice to meet you," I tried. "I met a woman a couple of days ago who was coming here for a rendezvous with her fiancé, you know. I gather he was a distant relation of the king's, and he was staying in a guest wing at the palace. Is that where we're going?"

"I am taking you to the women's quarters," Beshaam said, still sounding like she might jump and run away at any moment. "As my prince ordered."

"Great," I said. "The women's quarters? Yeah, I doubt Darian was staying there. Still, who wants a bunch of men ogling you when you're trying to sleep, right?"

For some reason, I thought of the night I'd spent camped in the dry riverbed, with soft snores coming from two of Gladya's escorts, while the third man kept silent watch over us.

Beshaam ignored my words, instead saying, "Are you hungry? If so I will have food sent once you are settled."

Between the interview with the vizier and the time spent waiting for a royal audience, hours had passed since the buttered bread I'd had this morning. "I could definitely eat, thanks," I told her.

She nodded, still without looking up. We exited the main part of the palace, crossing what seemed like a large courtyard, except that it was completely enclosed by the blank walls of tall buildings. There was only the set of doors we'd just come through, and a second pair straight ahead, flanked by more of the blade-wielding dark-skinned guards.

"The women's accommodations are here," Beshaam said, and paused nervously in front of the guards. One of them ran his gaze over first her, and then me. He gave a short nod and turned, unbarring the heavy doors and pulling one open.

I won't deny the odd little shiver of... something... that went through me as I entered. But I could hear the sound of feminine voices in easy conversation beyond, and the interior was only slightly less sumptuously appointed than the main palace had been.

Having guards isn't a bad thing, I reminded myself. There were probably loads of things in here that someone might want to steal. Valuable things. Of course the entrances would be guarded.

The door closed behind us with a noise of finality, the sound of a bar being dropped into place following a moment later.

FIVE

My eyes adjusted to the lower light, and I looked around as Beshaam led me along a hallway that opened onto a large communal space. The sounds of conversation ceased as the women seated around the room noticed my entrance and turned to look at me.

Apparently, the royal family had a lot of female guests. There were at least two dozen women in the room. All of them were attractive, dark haired, and dark-eyed. Were they members of the extended royal family, as Darian was? That would make sense, I supposed, especially since they gave off the air of knowing one another.

"Hello," I said into the awkward silence, lifting a hand and flickering my fingers in a tiny wave. There was no response beyond a few looks of consternation. They probably didn't get many blondes in here… or perhaps, many strangers.

"Come," Beshaam urged.

I let her lead me through the open area and into a hallway beyond, feeling eyes following me the whole way. I was already wishing I'd followed my gut and gone to the inn where Eldris and Aristede were staying.

The hall was lined with arched doorways on either side. Most had hanging cloths or curtains of beads covering them, obscuring what lay beyond.

A couple of them were open to my curious gaze, however, and revealed small but well-appointed rooms for sleeping.

"Would you care to bathe while food is prepared?" Beshaam asked.

In fact, that sounded heavenly. My rented room the previous night had only offered a small hand basin in which to wash, and I swore I could still feel sand and grit lodged in unfortunate places.

"I'd love that," I told her. "Can I help haul the water? I'd hate to put anyone out."

I knew that a place like this would be teeming with all sorts of servants, many of them strong men rather than tiny waifs like Beshaam. But still, the idea of simply assuming that someone would do the dirty work so I could laze in a tub rankled.

Beshaam's brow furrowed in confusion. "Haul... the water?"

"Carry buckets," I clarified.

Her face cleared, and she laughed—a nervous sound. "Oh, no need for anything like that. The bathing room is through here..."

It suddenly occurred to me that all of my belongings were sitting in a rented room some distance from the palace. I'd paid for several days' lodging up front, but even so, the idea of leaving everything there was a bit discomfiting. I opened my mouth to ask if there was anyway I could retrieve it, or perhaps send someone else to retrieve it, but the words stuck in my throat as I took in the chamber we'd just entered.

The entire back wall was a jumble of cracked stone, and I realized I was looking at the bones of the mountain against which the palace had been built. Water trickled from some of the cracks, pouring into a carved depression that, in turn, emptied into a huge stone basin. The basin overflowed from a spout on one edge, filling a second, smaller basin nestled against its side.

"You bathe in there," Beshaam said with a hint of condescension, pointing at the smaller tub. "The dirty water flows out and runs down the drainage system to a cistern. The kitchen servants use it to water the vegetable gardens during the dry season."

"Oh," I said, blinking.

In reality, it wasn't really all that much more impressive than the bathhouses in Rhyth, built over the city's hot springs. But in some ways, it was cleverer. Utrea was a dry land. The idea that they could divert part of a river indoors and use the wastewater to grow food was intriguing.

I frowned, a new thought hitting me. "Is it warm, or cold?"

Beshaam snorted, and I got the impression she was starting to relax around me a bit. "It's very, very cold," she said. "You use cold water for bathing during the spring, summer, and autumn. In winter, we'll sometimes bring in heated stones and put them in the bathing basin to warm it."

Ah, well. It *was* hot today. Funny… I'd grown up washing in a river more often than I'd washed in a tub. It had only taken a few months spent in Rhyth to spoil me for hot water, though.

"Got it," I said, reminding myself that the cold water would most likely be good for the red skin on my chest, which was already starting to itch and peel after my adventure in the desert.

The servant girl bustled around, gathering bathing supplies from niches hidden behind the bulk of the large basin. Figuring that I wasn't supposed to stand around like a lump of clay, I shrugged to myself and started disrobing. An instant later, Beshaam was there, silently helping undo the clasps and ties holding the draped fabric of my dress in place. As it fell away, she gave my reddened skin a frown.

"Your pale skin is not made for the sun," she observed, and then flushed as though she feared she'd offended me.

"The sun back home was never an issue," I told her dryly, "but, yeah, I think Utrea is closer to the sky or something. At midday, it's like standing too close to a cooking fire."

She made a tutting noise. "I have a mixture of beeswax and tallow here that might help with the peeling. The cool water should soothe the burns somewhat."

I smiled. "That's sweet of you," I said. "Honestly, though, it'll be fine in a couple of days."

I toed off my cloth slippers while Beshaam set the clothing neatly aside, and then dipped my fingers in the small pool. It was chilly, but not frigid. To be fair, I doubted *anything* in this land was frigid, at least during the summer.

"Go ahead," Beshaam urged, gesturing to the bath.

I sat on the edge, sliding my legs over. Bracing myself, I slipped into the water quickly, sitting down so I sank to my collarbones. My body erupted in gooseflesh, nipples hardening—but, on the positive side, at least I wasn't hot anymore. After a moment, the reaction faded, and I stood, the water coming just over my knees.

Before I could reach for the washrag and the lump of hard soap, Beshaam picked up the two items and dampened the cloth, working up a lather with the soap.

"Let me," she said. "It's part of my job."

Which… was… a bit weird. But, hey, different cultures, right?

"Uh… if you insist," I agreed. "Back home, we generally bathe ourselves, though."

"You are a under Prince Oblisii's roof, now," she said, as if that was an explanation.

Beshaam was detached as she washed me, but thorough. Like… *really* thorough, and I'll admit I blushed a bit as the cloth scrubbed over my breasts and sex.

"Rinse," she ordered, exposing a bossy streak now that she was in her element. I rinsed, and when I began to straighten, she shook her head. "No, stay down. I'll do your hair next."

Uneasiness hit me. Something still seemed decidedly off about this whole situation, and I wasn't ready to let Beshaam or anyone else here find the remaining gemstones hidden under my hair.

I lifted a hand, stopping her as she reached for a small pot containing a different kind of soap. "No, wait, Beshaam. Look, I don't mean to offend you, but, uh, you know how I said we didn't have other people bathe us back home? Well… there's… a custom among my people that… only a woman's parents or her bondmate can touch her hair."

There. That sounded totally reasonable. Didn't it?

Judging by the look Beshaam was giving me, it didn't, but I straightened my shoulders, ready to dig in on the issue.

"Oh," she said after an awkward pause. "Well. That's… odd. But I certainly don't mean to offend you either. Do you… want to wash your own hair? Or not wash it at all?"

Given how much dust and sand was in my hair, I was honestly pretty desperate to wash it. I decided that as long as I was careful not to put my back to her, she'd be unlikely to see any telltale glints of colored stone peeking through the strands.

"I'll do it," I said, extending my hand for the bowl of soft soap. "Again… sorry. I'd feel really, really uncomfortable letting you wash it, though. It's just… you know… the way I was raised."

She tried on a smile that mostly just made her look more confused, but she did pass me the soap. I hid my relieved sigh. The soap was interesting. It smelled exotic, and felt like whoever had made it had mixed some sort of light oil into it. I scrubbed at the heavy mass of my hair and rubbed the soap into my scalp before leaning back to swish the long strands through the water.

When I was done, my hair felt so smooth I didn't even think it would require additional hair oil to prevent tangles. Surreptitiously, I let my fingers dig into the wet length at the back of my skull, counting the tiny braids hidden underneath and feeling for the chains holding my last remaining currency. Reassured, I lifted my head and shook the water out of my ears.

"There we are," I told Beshaam a bit too brightly. "All done, no assistance needed."

She pasted on a polite smile and met me with a large towel as I stepped out, drying me with particular care in the sunburned areas. As promised, she retrieved a pot of ointment and smeared it across the worst of the red areas while I took the towel and patted the excess water from my hair.

In Beshaam's defense, the ointment really was kind of soothing.

She truly did seem to be a nice girl; it was just the situation that was putting me off. And aside from the rather ominous *clunk* of the doors being barred behind us, I couldn't have said precisely what about it was bothering me. I was a guest in the royal palace while the prince investigated an attack on me in the desert, for the gods' sakes. Lots of people would give their right eyetooth for that kind of honor.

Beshaam helped me get back in my dress with the same efficiency she'd used to help me get out of it. I ran my fingers through my damp tresses a few more times to untangle them, before pulling the hair at my temples and the top of my head into a messy braid that would keep it out of my face while it dried. If it also provided another layer of hair to shield against any possible glint of a gemstone, well... so much the better.

Once I was more-or-less put together again, Beshaam led me back through the hallway full of sleeping rooms, stopping before one of the ones I'd noticed earlier with the cloth hanging pulled back out of the way.

"This is your private chamber," she said.

I wasn't sure that a room with no real door on it counted as *private*, but I thanked her and wandered inside, looking around. There was a bed that looked larger than one might have expected for a single person. Also, a sort of long, low table with a polished metal mirror on it, set against the wall. A chair sat in front of the mirror, and on either side of it were shelves, cunningly integrated into the table's legs. Those shelves were covered in vials, bottles, and tiny stone pots with cork stoppers. Another little table sat next to the bed, with an oil lamp on top.

"Erm, it's very nice," I said, aware that with my silence, I was in danger of looking crass. "What are all the little bottles and things?"

"Oils and creams for your skin, mostly," Beshaam said, as though surprised I had to ask. "There's also perfume, kohl, and other pigments for your lips and cheeks."

I also noticed a comb and a pig-bristle hairbrush sitting by the mirror, along with a selection of hair ornaments and ties. Wow. Apparently, the women in Safaad were *really* serious about personal care.

"That's... very impressive," I hazarded. "Sometimes the priests back home use kohl around their eyes for important ceremonies. The rest of us… don't really tend to paint our faces." *Unless it's warriors going into battle*, I didn't add, since that seemed impolitic.

Beshaam only shrugged. "Women in the palace like to make themselves look pretty before being seen by the prince, or the king."

I felt my forehead wrinkle in a frown. *And painting their faces makes them look pretty?*

I flopped down to sit on the edge of the bed and let it go. "All right. I'll keep it in mind."

She smiled the same *I'm-confused-but-trying-not-to-offend-you* smile from earlier. "Do you require anything else? The servants should be here with the evening meal in an hour or so."

Any response I might have made was interrupted by a shadow crossing the doorway. I looked up to see a tall, strikingly beautiful woman step inside, looking around the chamber as if she owned the place. Her raven-black hair was piled atop her head in intricately woven braids that coiled like snakes.

Her chiseled features were haughty, from her kohl-lined mahogany eyes to her cruel, painted lips. I could swear that I saw a hint of gold dust glittering on her high cheekbones, as well. Her body had the spare grace of a dancer, but the slim lines of her arms and legs spoke of someone who had never done an honest day's labor in her life. She raked her gaze over me from head to toe with what could only be described as disdain.

Politeness dictated that I rise and introduce myself, but something about that superior stare rankled me. Instead, I stayed where I was, perched on the edge of the bed with my weight resting on my hands as I held her gaze, not backing down. It was obvious she expected me to speak first, and I won't deny my small flash of satisfaction at her growing irritation as I let the silence stretch, my eyebrows raised in a silent question.

Beshaam cleared her throat nervously. "Lady Lesimba, this is Frella of Drae—"

"Quiet, girl," the woman said. Her voice was low and throaty. "Did anyone give you leave to speak?"

I straightened from my careless slouch, feeling my temper rise. "*Excuse me.* She has *my* leave to speak, and it's not polite to interrupt."

The woman—Lesimba—sneered openly. "Perhaps in your land, they allow servants to speak out of turn. What was your name, again? Fretta?"

"Frella," I ground out. "Now, what, pray tell, can I do for you, *Lady Lesimba*?"

This was not shaping up to be my finest moment of diplomacy, I was aware. But few things were quicker to rouse me than the privileged shitting all over the less privileged. I hadn't liked her on first sight, but by treating Beshaam like dirt, this woman had just ensured that any respect I might have shown her was tipped straight out the window.

Not that there was, you know, a window in here.

Lesimba looked at me as though I were an insect that had just crawled into her soup bowl. "You are new here. I wished to meet my husband's latest plaything. I am Prince Oblisii's First Wife."

"Nice to meet you," I growled, with all the sincerity that you might expect by that point. "Though you'll be relieved to know, I'm only here long enough to have a second meeting with your husband, and then I'll be out of your hair."

Lesimba's eyes raked over me from head to foot, and I wondered if she'd learned that way of staring through a person's clothing from Oblisii.

"Foolish girl," she said. "I will wait until my prince decides whether to keep you or not before ensuring that you learn your place. In the mean time, stay out of my way and your life will go much easier."

With that, she pivoted on one neatly slippered foot and left the room, the door hanging swishing in the breeze of her exit as I blinked after her in consternation.

"Wow," I mused. "What a vicious cow." I caught Beshaam's flinch out of the corner of my eye and turned to her, frowning. "Sorry. I get that she's your boss, but… just… *wow*."

The young servant had gone a bit pale beneath her golden skin. "Please do not speak so. You would do well not to antagonize her."

I raised an eyebrow. "I realize that little exchange wasn't one of my finest moments, Beshaam, but like I told her, I'll be out of here soon. Probably tomorrow."

Beshaam cringed in on herself, and her voice was barely audible when she said, "No. You won't be."

I stared at her. "Excuse me?"

She swallowed hard. "The prince had you brought to the *women's' quarters.*" She gave me a significant look, as though willing me to understand what she was *really* saying.

"Er... yes?" I allowed, knowing that I was missing some vitally important subtext here. An unpleasant sinking feeling began to take up residence in my stomach.

Beshaam stared at me, clearly hoping I would somehow soak up the information like a dishrag, so she wouldn't have to say it aloud. Eventually, she broke.

"This is where Prince Oblisii keeps his wives and concubines," she finally blurted.

SIX

"Um..." I said, playing for time while I ran Beshaam's words over in my mind a couple more times to make sure I'd heard right.

"He *chose* you," she said, staring at me with wide eyes.

I stared back.

And then I brushed past her without a word, shoving the door hanging out of my way so I could stride out of the room, back down the hallway, through the communal area to the big double doors. Once there, I pounded on them with my fist. Beshaam hadn't followed me—or if she had, she was hanging back while I pummeled the thick wood. I could sense other eyes on me, though. Apparently I was putting on a show for all the other wives.

Concubines.

Whatever.

There was the sound of a heavy bar being lifted, and one of the doors creaked open to reveal the broad body of a stony-faced guard. He stared down at me from his considerable advantage of height, clearly unimpressed.

"I'm leaving now," I said, and took one step into the open doorway.

At which point my chest mashed against the two crossed staves that had appeared in front of me as if by magic. The corners of the first guard's mouth turned down in a distinctly displeased way. I took a single step back.

Soft hands closed around my upper arm and tugged me away from the door. "You mustn't," Beshaam whispered, before turning to look up at the towering guards. "She didn't know," she added in a louder voice.

The doors closed, and I heard the bar being dropped in place once more.

I met Beshaam's worried brown eyes. "Tell me," I began in a terribly serious voice, "exactly what the *fuck* is going on here. Are all of these women prisoners?"

"No," she said quickly.

"Then what was that about?" I asked, gesturing at the door with an out-flung arm.

"Not here," she muttered, and dragged me away from the watching eyes of the other women. She didn't lead me back to the questionable privacy of the bedchamber, but instead, brought me to a little storage area beyond the bathing chamber.

It was dark and deserted, and I rounded on her. "Talk, Beshaam. The other women aren't prisoners, but I am? I'm not staying here. I didn't sign up to be some creepy nobleman's plaything. I only came here to report a crime!"

"You can't leave," Beshaam said, her expression still frightened. "The other women are already established as the prince's wives or concubines. But the guards know you are new, and still await the prince's pleasure. They will not allow you to leave before he makes his final decision to accept you or not."

"*His* final decision?" I nearly squeaked. "What about *my* final decision? What about my *initial* decision, for that matter?"

Beshaam shrank back from my anger. She seemed to do a lot of that sort of thing, I noticed. The rosy picture of Safaad I'd been assembling in my head was growing ever more tarnished.

"It is considered a great honor even to be considered for a place in the prince's harem," she said.

"*Not by me.*" I bit off each word sharply. "I'm getting out of here."

I thought longingly of the Purple Cloak... of the two men who would be waiting there if I could get out of this madhouse somehow and return to them. I barely knew them, yet where the mere thought of Prince Oblisii made my skin crawl, thoughts of Eldris' gleaming white smile and Aristede's sly humor made longing rise in my chest. Hell, at this point I'd even put up with Rayth's look of haughty disapproval if it meant getting away from here.

Beshaam still appeared deeply worried on my behalf. "You can't cause trouble, Lady Frella. The prince will be coming in the next day or two to claim you as his and decide if he wishes to keep you. If he hears that you've been making problems for the guards, it will go worse for you." Her voice grew quieter on the last sentence, as though the words physically pained her.

"Claim me," I echoed, my voice flat. "As in...?"

Her eyes slid down and to the side. "To... take your maidenhead. It is his right, as a noble."

I continued to stare. "Beshaam. I'm twenty-two years old. Why in the gods' names would you expect me to still be a virgin?"

Her eyes flew to mine, appalled. In fact, she was openly gaping at me, her jaw going slack for a moment before she caught herself and snapped it shut.

"You're... not...?" She swallowed and tried again. "Lady Frella—if you don't bleed... if the prince suspects you of not being pure..."

I frowned. "What does bleeding during sex have to do with being pure? What does 'pure' even *mean* in this context?"

"If he suspects you are not a virgin, he will send you to live with the women that the lesser nobles and palace soldiers amuse themselves with!" The words came out in a rush.

"*Lovely,*" I said, my voice gone flat again.

Tears pooled in Beshaam's eyes, and a flash of bitter anger flitted across her face. It was the first hint of spirit I'd seen from her.

"My younger sister ended up in such a place," she whispered. "She killed herself not long after."

That stopped me cold. "Beshaam," I said. "What are you even doing here? Are *you* a prisoner?"

Her expression wavered as though it might crumple, but she controlled it. "I am... and I am not. I could leave the palace, but this is a far better life than anything I could aspire to beyond its walls. I have no father, and my mother was a prostitute. The old queen granted me a place as a servant. Since she was executed, I have few friends here. There is very little standing between me and my sister's fate."

My voice and face softened. "You could leave and travel to a different city, Beshaam. Start over somewhere new."

She met my eyes and quirked an eyebrow. "Really? With no money and no horse? How would I go about doing that, Lady Frella?"

There was no mistaking the irony lacing her tone, and I felt shame well up. How easy it was to forget that not everyone was as lucky as I had been in this life. Not everyone had status and wealth. Not everyone had jewels woven into their hair. I made a sudden decision. It might well turn out to be a foolish one, but I was going to do it anyway.

I reached under my honey-colored curls and untangled a chain. It was difficult after bathing and letting my hair dry into messy ringlets. In a few moments, though, I was able to extract one of the gems.

"Take this," I said. "Help me figure out a way to get out of here, and then you do the same."

Her eyes grew wide. "That's why you wouldn't let me wash your hair!"

"Got it in one," I said wryly. "So, do we have a deal?"

Beshaam's mouth opened and closed a few times as she tried to come to terms with this new development. I guess it was kind of a big thing to drop on her out of the blue. Had she honestly considered herself lucky to be stuck in a life of bathing and clothing other people, accepting abuse from those in power? Maybe she didn't *want* to leave, I realized.

"We have a deal," she said in a tiny voice, and I relaxed.

She accepted the green gemstone set in its gold clasp on the short chain. For a moment, she stood frozen, staring at the glinting thing in her palm, but then she quickly transferred it to an inner pocket in her plain dress. I could only imagine what would befall her if she were caught with such a thing before she escaped the palace. No doubt Lesimba would take utter glee in accusing her of theft.

"Now," I said. "How do I get out?"

Beshaam pursed her lips, thinking. "The doors are always guarded, day and night. The guards are loyal; only the most trusted men are assigned to the women's quarters, for obvious reasons."

"I'm surprised they don't use eunuchs," I muttered.

Beshaam wrinkled her nose. "Eunuchs are weak. And no soldier would agree to such a thing."

"My brother is a eunuch," I said tiredly. "And so is one of my adoptive fathers."

Beshaam gave me another one of those *looks*— the 'what the hell kind of crazy place do you come from' look—and I sighed, letting it go.

"Never mind," I said. "So, the door is guarded. Windows?"

She winced, but then looked thoughtful. "They are small, and high off the ground. But... maybe you could figure out a way to climb up to one?" Her expression wavered back towards doubt. "We're on the side of a mountain, though. The windows are all on the side facing the cliff. You would also have to climb down the mountain somehow. It would be very dangerous. I don't know that you could do it."

"Aren't there any other doors?" I asked bleakly.

"None. The prince takes the security of the women's quarters very seriously."

My mouth twisted. "Window it is, then. What's the best one to try?"

Her expression turned unhappy. "Probably in the communal room. You should wait until late at night, when the women are asleep."

And hope that Oblisii doesn't decide to stop by and take my non-existent maidenhead before then, I thought bitterly.

"Sure," I said. "Thanks for your help. You should get out of here, so you're not around to get in trouble when they find out I've scarpered. Can you do that?"

She nodded slowly. "My duties will be done by nightfall." She hesitated. "I... could... wait for you?"

I smiled, though it was grim. "Best not. I seem to have become a lodestone for trouble these past few days. I'm guessing the prince will be far more interested in finding me once he figures out what happened than he will be in finding you."

Her eyebrows drew together, and she nodded. "It may be days before anyone thinks to wonder about my whereabouts. Here, I am not Beshaam to most people. I am only a girl, like all the other girls who serve."

I reached out and cupped her cheek. "Well, you'll always be Beshaam to me. Stay safe, and thank you for helping."

She drew her full lower lip between her teeth, staring up at me with large brown eyes. "Thank you for buying my freedom. But I fear I've only pointed you toward danger."

I forced a too-broad smile. "Nonsense. You've pointed me toward *adventure*. I'm all about adventure—just ask anyone who knows me." I glanced down at my fancy dress. "Though I sort of wish I'd worn breeches under this thing now. Anyway, go do whatever you're supposed to be doing. I'm going to try to stay out of everybody's way until they go to bed. Especially bitch-face—I mean, Lesimba."

"She's dangerous," Beshaam said. "Don't cross her again."

I thought of Lesimba's slender arms and legs… her lack of muscle definition. The bandits on the road might've bested me. Fucking *Rayth* might've bested me. But if it came down to it, I could take Lesimba. The thought made a grim smile slide over my lips.

Still, after watching her cold eyes running over me, you wouldn't catch me eating or drinking anything in this place before I left. I could picture her slipping poison into a cup a lot more easily than I could picture her attacking me in an open fight.

"Don't you worry about me, Beshaam," I said. "I intend to get out of here safely. I've got places to go and people to see."

⚜

I spent the rest of the day hiding in the storage area, until a different servant girl wandered in and gave a squeak of surprise when she found me sitting on a table in the corner with my ankles crossed, dozing while I waited for night to come. I gave her a friendly smile and wandered out, poking my head into the bathing chamber as I passed it.

It was empty, so I slaked my thirst with the cool mountain spring water. Figuring that the girl must have come to ready a bath for one of the others, I didn't linger. I'd been avoiding my room in hopes of also avoiding Lesimba that way, but I went there now. I guessed that the others were probably eating at this time of day. When I heard the sounds of people entering the hallway full of bedchambers, I got in bed, doused the lamp, and pulled the covers over me, pretending to already be asleep.

Some time later, I saw the drape across the doorway swish to one side, a figure silhouetted against the flickering light from the hall. I was certain it was Lesimba, but I remained still and silent as I feigned slumber. My skin crawled with disquiet as she stood there for long moments. Eventually, to my relief, she let the drape fall and continued to her own room.

Time crawled. I wasn't sure exactly how late I should let it get before making my move. I ended up waiting until everything was quiet and still except for the occasional snore or rustle from one of the other rooms… and then waited some more. I thought it must be well after midnight when I finally sat up in bed and took stock.

There was barely any light. They must have put out most of the lamps and candles when the last people went to bed. I could make out gray shapes in the unfamiliar room, but no details. My fingers ran over the woven sheets I was lying on. They felt too delicate to work safely as rope, while the single blanket was too thick and coarse to be useful that way. I didn't want to make noise by trying to tear them, so I left them behind with a sigh and crept toward the door.

The cloth hanging across it was the same flimsy weave as the sheets — no use there. It looked like I was doomed to do whatever I was going to do without a rope. *Lucky me.*

A single lamp flickered wildly on the large table in the communal area, the flame guttering as the oil ran out. I grabbed another unlit lamp from nearby and topped it off, looking around as the flame grew stronger. I hadn't taken as much heed of the room as I should have on the two occasions I'd been in here, but as my eyes slid over the chairs, tables, and divans, an idea took shape.

I just hoped that the other women turned out to be heavy sleepers.

There were three windows on the side of the room to the right of the big double doors.

Fortunately, those doors were heavy as well as tall and wide, or else I'd probably need to worry more about rousing the guards than rousing the sleeping wives and concubines. The bottom ledges of the windows were perhaps twice my height from the ground, or a bit more.

I chose the middle window, because why not, and looked around for the sturdiest table that I thought I could move on my own. When it was in place under the window with a bare minimum of screeching legs and unladylike grunting, I found two identical chairs with heavy frames. A third, lighter chair, straddled the seats of the first two after I lifted them onto the table, facing each other. Finally, I balanced a stool precariously on the seat of the third chair and stepped back to inspect the small mountain of furniture.

Yeah, this was either going to work brilliantly, or I was going to break my neck. But, on the bright side, if I couldn't climb up a rickety tower of tables and chairs and haul myself through the tiny window above... well, that probably meant I didn't have any business trying to climb down the sheer palace wall and the cliff face that lay beyond.

SEVEN

I didn't have any business trying to climb down the wall and the cliff face. How terribly surprising. Though, to be honest, I was a bit proud of my upper body strength after successfully hauling myself through the narrow window. It had still been a little way above shoulder height when I balanced precariously on the stool at the top of the furniture pile. I was pretty sure that stupid Lesimba couldn't have managed it with her twiggy arms, anyway.

So, now I was perched on the sill with my upper body outside and my legs dangling inside, taking stock in the weak moonlight. Ever since I'd tumbled down a rocky cliff-side in the hills beyond Draebard when I was a little girl, I was… less than sanguine about heights. I'd escaped that time with nothing more than a sprained ankle and some scrapes, but I didn't think I'd be so lucky if I were stupid enough to try going down the smooth wall below me. Far from it.

Smooth might be a bit of a misnomer, but there was a huge difference between pockmarks in stone and actual hand- and footholds that you could, y'know, *hold*. The palace wall definitely had more of the former than the latter. I let my gaze sweep wider, taking in all of my surroundings. I needed to do *something*, unless I wanted to be found sitting up here like a fool by the first person to come wandering into the common room.

If *down* wasn't going to be an option, that left *up*.

The high windows were set right beneath the room's ceiling. If I reached up, I could grasp the edge of the roof with my fingertips. I got the best grip I could and used it to keep from plunging to my death as I scrambled up to stand on the sill, instead of sitting on it. Now I had a great view of the exterior of one of the domed ceilings I'd so admired earlier. But, more importantly, there was a flat area extending all the way around the edge—and it was wide enough to walk on.

My arms were going to be really, *really* sore tomorrow, I could tell. I gritted my teeth and pulled myself up to the flat area, wincing as I heard the material of my pretty dress tear. My heart was pounding by the time I belly-flopped onto the gritty stone, and I stared at a pile of bird droppings I'd nearly face-planted into. *Eww.*

So. Now I was on the roof. That constituted progress, right?

It was kind of interesting from an architectural standpoint, the way the domes meshed together like a giant honeycomb. Unfortunately, the steep surfaces of the interlocking domes meant I was restricted to the narrow ledge winding around the outside of the roof. I thought the flat area must have been designed so that the builders would have something solid to stand on while they were working. They probably hadn't added it with future runaway concubines in mind, but at this point, I would take what I could get.

In the absence of whatever system of ladders and platforms had allowed those long-ago builders access to the roof, it was likely that my only way down would be another conveniently placed window. I needed someplace that was on the other side of the locked door leading to the women's quarters. That part was easy enough, since the only windows I'd seen while I was inside were the three in the common room.

However, I also needed to be someplace where people came and went frequently. Wriggling into a locked storeroom — or a locked anything — wouldn't help me very much. I peered cautiously over the edge of the walkway, trying to see what sorts of window options were available along this stretch. Then I remembered how much I didn't like heights, and decided I would be better served by lying on my stomach in the dried bird droppings while I looked for windows. That way, I could inch my head over the edge and look down without feeling like I was going to topple off.

It took four such attempts at window reconnaissance before the smell of bread and lingering smoke from the previous day's cooking fires let me know I'd found the kitchens. Kitchens were good. People and things went in and out of kitchens all the time, but not usually in the dark hours between midnight and dawn.

Perfect.

Now I just had to get through that window without dying. But I'd gotten out of the last window successfully… so, how hard could it be?

⌐ ♕ ¬

Some considerable time later, I sat on the floor of the kitchen nursing a shallow cut on my ankle and maybe, just maybe, trembling a tiny bit. For future reference, asking how hard something could be was apparently a good way to rouse the gods' ire. Do not, under any circumstances, ask how hard something could possibly be before attempting to do it.

Also, don't wear expensive, gauzy dresses while attempting to gain clandestine access to or from a roof. They're completely impractical. The floofy parts get in your way when you're climbing, and they tear easily. Less than four full days spent in Utrea, and I was already getting very tired of wearing torn clothing.

Fortunately, there had been a convenient wooden countertop beneath the window, so I didn't have to drop all the way to the floor. Unfortunately, it was a kitchen, so there had been several knives lying on the aforementioned countertop. I'd avoided most of them. In fact, I'd avoided all of them except the one that had flipped up and cut my ankle when my foot landed on the handle.

Boots and breeches for rooftop escapes, not gauzy dresses — just saying.

Anyway, the cut didn't look bad enough to warrant anything more than tying a strip of my torn skirt around it to keep from bleeding on the king's nice, clean kitchen floor. Once I was done sitting on the aforementioned floor and shaking for a few minutes, I tied off the makeshift bandage around my hurt ankle and got up to explore. By that time, my eyes had adjusted to the darkness enough to find a candle and flint striker sitting on a worktable.

The flickering illumination showed a truly vast space — probably necessary when you were trying to feed an entire castle full of people three times a day. The doors didn't appear to be guarded, but I wanted a more concrete plan before I ventured into unknown territory. I was still inside the palace complex, which seemed almost like its own little city inside the city.

I needed to be outside of the walls. There, I'd be free to return to my rented room and get my belongings. I'd be free to go to the Purple Cloak and try to get help.

My eyes fell on the cart of towels and linens parked in one corner of the large room. It was quite possible there was a laundry inside the palace as well. Still, it gave me an idea. There was one place where carts of goods would enter and leave the palace grounds on a regular basis. The stables. That was where I needed to be. I would sneak into the stables and find an outbound wagon to hide in.

Plan in place, I extinguished the candle and waited for my eyes to adjust again. The kitchen had an exterior set of double doors where produce and other supplies were presumably delivered. Those doors were barred on the inside, but no one had worried about people trying to break *out* of the kitchen—only trying to break *into* it. I unbarred them and crept outside, where the moon was starting to slide low in the west.

It wasn't difficult to follow the path taken by carts delivering supplies. Countless wheels had left ruts as they passed along the same route, day in and day out. I hugged the shadows as I approached a low building from which I could detect the scent of animals and manure. After growing up as a village girl, I'd never quite gotten used to city dwellers' preference for keeping horses inside buildings instead of outdoor pens. As stables went, though, this appeared to be a very nice one.

Movement caught my eye, and I flattened against the nearest wall as a bored looking guard wandered past. I waited until he rounded a corner, out of sight, and darted across the open space to my target. With luck, the carts would be kept somewhere out-of-the-way enough that I could find one already loaded in preparation for heading out, and hide in it until morning.

I silently urged fate to present me with a nice wagon full of sacks, maybe with a tarpaulin pulled over the bed for good measure. I found the collection of wagons and carriages on the opposite end of the building. They were all neatly parked and well maintained, another example of the efficiency of this place. Really, it seemed to be a great place to live as long as you weren't a servant girl, or a prostitute, or a random blonde-haired woman who happened to catch the eye of a creepy prince with entitlement issues.

Inside the stables, I could hear restless snorts from the animals. I wandered between the carts, trying to decide which was most likely to be leaving first. They all looked... empty. Which I supposed made sense, though it certainly wasn't very helpful.

"Who are you?" said a male voice, close enough to me that I jumped and barely managed to swallow my squeak of surprise.

It was a pleasant tenor, not loud, and it was attached to a pleasant-faced man about my age. He was holding a coiled whip in one hand and a lantern in the other; staring at me with consternation and worry fighting for dominance on his features.

"No one," I said immediately, the words tumbling out of my mouth oh-so-smoothly.

Brilliant, Frella. Nothing suspicious there.

"Who are you?" I asked before he could reply — taking the offensive.

The young man blinked. "I'm Nyx," he said, still in that soft voice I had to strain a bit to hear. "What are you doing out here, my lady?"

His eyes strayed from my face to my bound ankle and torn skirt, pausing on the way back up. I flushed and grabbed the material together where the skin of my bare hip must've been showing through one of the ripped places.

"Nothing," I said sharply. Because that was *sure* to allay his suspicions. I had to squash the urge to roll my eyes at myself.

"It doesn't look like nothing, my lady," Nyx said, and I scowled at the hint of humor I thought I heard in that quiet voice.

At least he was pleasant to look at, even if he was secretly laughing at me. I studied him closer, taking in messy, short-cropped black hair, olive skin, and lean muscles. He was decently tall, but something about the way he held himself made him look smaller than he actually was—like he was hunching his shoulders. He tilted his head, studying me right back, and the light from the lantern fell on a dark bruise marring his high cheekbone.

I scowled, and he shifted uncomfortably in place.

"My lady?" he asked again. From his mode of dress and the horsewhip he was carrying in lieu of a proper weapon, he was clearly a stable hand. His eyes darted around as though he were nervous for some reason, and something inside me decided it wanted to trust him even though I had no worldly reason to do so. He looked at me again, his eyes meeting mine briefly as he said, "Come inside. The guards will be passing by on their rounds soon."

The evidence that he wanted to help me avoid the patrols sealed the deal. He led me into the faintly stuffy warmth of the stables, pressing a finger to his lips to signal for quiet and pointing to a second lad asleep in a chair near the door. I followed him down the line of horses tied in stalls, their rumps facing us, tails flicking as we passed.

He took me all the way to the other end of the building, where a smaller door led into a room full of saddles, bridles, and harnesses. After closing the door behind us, he carefully placed the lit lantern on a stool and turned back to me.

"If we stay quiet, no one will hear us talking in here," he said. "Now, again, what are you doing out here in the middle of the night with your dress torn and your ankle bound up? Are you hurt?"

I rolled my lower lip between my teeth, chewing on it as the part of my mind that instinctively wanted to trust him and the part insisting that doing so would be foolish bickered silently. His dark brows drew together in worry, their graceful sweep like birds' wings. In this light, the purple and green mottling on the side of his face stood out sharply.

I spoke before the conscious decision to do so registered. "I'm in trouble. I came here yesterday morning to seek an audience with the king. Prince Oblisii was there, and he had me taken to stay in the women's quarters. I thought he was offering me accommodations for the night, but it turns out he was offering me a place in his harem." My lips twisted. "Though *offering* isn't the right word, since I wasn't given any choice in the matter. One of the servants warned me that he'd be coming to claim me before long, so I climbed out of a window, pulled myself onto the roof, and escaped."

At the mention of Oblisii's name, something dark passed over Nyx's handsome features. "That was stupid," he said, his voice even softer and harder to hear than it had been before. "You could have gotten killed doing that."

My fists balled at my hips. "Yeah? Well, given the choice between falling to my death and what was supposedly going to happen when Oblisii showed up and realized I haven't been a virgin since I was sixteen, I figured I'd take my chances."

"Ah," he said.

"*Ah*," I echoed sarcastically. "So, here I am, still stuck inside the palace walls, looking for a way to smuggle myself out in a wagon or something."

"You need to get out right away," he said. "When the prince finds out what you did, he'll be furious."

I threw my hands up in disgust. "You *think*?"

He shook his head, clearly frustrated with my theatrics. "Your plan won't work. The carts may not go out at all today. And most of the ones that do are empty when they leave to pick up supplies. There'd be no place for you to hide."

Well, *fuck*.

A thought occurred to me. "How'd you even know I was out there, anyway? I was being quiet..."

His mouth twitched. "The horses got restless. They knew something was going on outside."

That made sense. I hadn't even thought of it.

"And you're... what?" I prodded. "On overnight guard duty or something?"

"No. Rendell was supposed to be watching things tonight. The boy we passed in the chair. I... uh... I don't always sleep the best." His eyes slid away again. I wished I could get a better look at their color. Earlier, I thought the lantern light had illuminated a flash of green, but now they just looked brown.

I raised an eyebrow. "Doesn't seem like Rendell shares that particular problem."

He gave a little huff of laughter, flinching afterward as though the small expression of amusement had taken him by surprise.

"So," I began, "are you going to drag me back to the women's quarters, or what?"

Without weapons, I didn't think I could overpower him, and with my torn skirts flapping and my stupid cloth slippers, I doubted I could outrun him, either.

"No," he said, "I already told you. You need to get out of here before they find out you're gone." he paused, as though debating with himself. "Look, there's a way out of the palace grounds that not many people know about. I'll show you, but we have to hurry."

Relief flooded me at the knowledge that he wasn't going to raise the alarm or hand me over to the guards. "Thank you," I breathed.

His jaw worked for a moment, and I watched the tendons moving, mesmerized. I really, really wanted a closer view of those soulful eyes. I blinked, dragging my wits back together as he spoke.

"Don't thank me yet." The words were still low-pitched, but his tone turned grim. "Let's get you out safely first."

EIGHT

Nyx's secret way out of the palace grounds turned out to be an old drainage tunnel with a broken metal grate on the far end. "It's mostly dry at this time of year," he'd murmured, and I tried not to cringe as my pretty blue slippers squished in the muck that even summer's lack of rain hadn't eliminated.

Apparently, the city of Safaad was riddled with tunnels like these. Without them, Nyx explained, flooding would be rampant during the spring rains. Drains placed throughout the city directed the runoff away from the buildings and roads, into a lake above the agricultural lands that nestled at the base of the mountains.

Again, I was impressed by the Utreans' mastery of their limited water resources. It simply wasn't something we worried about on Eburos. Yes, some parts of the island were drier than others, but people just settled around the river basins where water was plentiful. We didn't try to change the land to suit us.

Unfortunately, the reality of this feat of Utrean engineering was... unpleasant. The mud—at least, I was telling myself it was mud—bred insects, and the smell was reminiscent of a dirty animal pen right after a rainstorm. That being said, if it disgorged us someplace quiet—and outside the palace walls—I'd celebrate the sacrifice of the dainty slippers with a flagon of ale and a prayer to the gods.

Nyx's heavy boots were far better suited to our surroundings, but the uneven, slippery footing exposed a certain carefulness to his gait that I hadn't noticed back at the stables. It wasn't just his hunched shoulders; he was carrying himself like someone who'd been beaten recently.

Maybe not a shock, given the bruising on his face—but the realization gave me pause nonetheless. I kept my mouth shut as we walked, both to keep the flies and the stench *out*, and to keep anything stupid that I might have been tempted to say *in*.

At least until we reached the broken grate and squeezed through the tight gap between the iron bars, emerging into a dry gully. I scanned our surroundings, and sure enough, the edges of Safaad glittered a short distance away to our left— street lamps twinkling merrily in the dark.

"We made it!" I exclaimed.

A stupid grin slid over my face. Without thinking, I flung my arms around Nyx's shoulders and pressed a sloppy kiss to his unbruised cheek. He stiffened and I let him go, chagrined—unsure if I'd irritated an unseen injury, or if I'd offended him somehow with my show of effusiveness.

He tried on a smile, but it couldn't cover the sudden paleness of his face. "Of course we did. Are you all right on your own now? I have to get back or they'll realize I'm gone. The market square is just beyond those buildings at the top of the rise."

A sinking feeling assailed me at the idea of my battered rescuer disappearing back into that fetid tunnel. But that was ridiculous, I tried to tell myself. Why should the idea of saying goodbye to someone I'd only met an hour ago upset me? It wasn't as though I were likely to see Beshaam again, or Gladya, or the man I'd chatted with at the palace... gods, I couldn't even remember his name, and that had only been yesterday. Why was Nyx any different? And yet—

"Come with me," I said impulsively.

He blinked in surprise, and the lantern caught that unusual flash of green again for an instant. "I can't," he said.

Stubbornness pricked at the edges of my emotions. "Yes you can." I caught his eyes. Made him look at me. "Tell me those injuries you're trying to hide came from a fractious colt. Tell me they came from a brawl, and not from a beating."

He didn't look away, but something slid across his eyes like a curtain lowering. "The stable master is too fond of drink. Sometimes the rest of us pay the price for it."

I watched him, trying to understand.

"If you have a way out of the palace—" I gestured at the tunnel. "—then why don't you leave?"

That curtain still hung across his expression, stymieing my attempts to read him in the flickering light.

"Having a livelihood and a roof is better than starving on the streets again," he said eventually.

"It's better than wandering in the mountains, trying to live on berries and twigs."

"So get a different job," I said. "You can't tell me there aren't liveries and private stables in need of strong workers."

His lip twitched into a twisted smile that disappeared before I could decipher it. "Safaad runs on a guild system. Apprenticeships come through family ties, and I haven't had any of those in…" He trailed off and swallowed. "In a very long time. I have to go. Will you be all right?"

No, damn it. I *wouldn't* be all right, knowing that Nyx was trudging back to the master who beat him because he thought he had no place else to go. No other options. I gritted my teeth, uneasy with doing this twice in one day. But I was still going to do it.

I turned my back to Nyx and swept my hair to the side. On some level, I was aware that he could easily rip the chains free from their golden braids, shove me to the ground, and run off with my only remaining valuables… yet I felt not the slightest flicker of worry at baring my secret to him.

I heard his sharp intake of breath, and let my hair fall as I turned back to him.

"We won't starve," I said softly, "and I have friends in the city. Now. *Come with me.*"

"Why?" he breathed.

I tipped my head, studying his handsome features. "You were willing to help me. Why shouldn't I help you?"

He was staring at me like he'd never seen anything like me, and I finally got a proper look at those arresting eyes of his. I'd been right on both counts. They were an earthy shade of brown, but green rings surrounded his irises. An entire forest hidden inside his gaze.

"All right," he whispered. "I'll come."

I led him back to the boarding house where I'd rented a room, feeling conspicuous in my torn and muddy clothing as we walked down the quiet roadways. Safaad's citizenry might have been asleep, but the guards that patrolled the streets were not. A pair of them slowed upon seeing us as we approached the boarding house, and I felt Nyx tense beside me.

Thinking fast, I looped my arm through his and leaned on him, staggering a bit as though drunk. Nyx's breath caught in surprise, but one of the guards laughed and nudged the other knowingly. With a final smirk in my direction, he prodded his comrade into motion again and they resumed their patrol.

With relief, I steered Nyx through the doorway and let him go, blowing out a breath as my tension eased. The landlord was doubtless abed, but he'd left a lamp burning on the counter and there were several unlit candles set nearby. Nyx extinguished the lantern, which had started flickering as it ran out of oil. I grabbed a candle and lit it from the lamp, using it to light our way up to my room.

Nothing inside had been disturbed, and my shoulders slumped as the rest of my worry slid away. I set the candle on the little table and flopped onto the edge of the bed as reaction set in.

"Well, that was fun," I said in a faux-cheerful tone. "We should totally do things like that more often."

Nyx hovered near the door. "If those guards remember seeing you once the call goes out that you've escaped the prince's harem, they'll know exactly where to come. Your hair is rather... distinctive."

I sighed. "Yes, I know. Let me change into something that doesn't have gaping holes in it, and we'll leave. Like I said, I've got friends in the city. They're staying at the Purple Cloak. We can go there."

"It's almost dawn," Nyx said. "We should hurry."

Really, all I wanted to do—now that the immediate crisis was over—was to fall back on the mattress and sleep for about a day straight. "All right," I said instead, and pushed myself upright on aching muscles.

I hadn't unpacked yesterday's purchases of clothing and supplies, which was just as well. I rummaged in the knapsack I'd stowed them in until I found a practical thigh-length tunic and breeches, along with a clean pair of stockings.

"Turn around, unless you want a free show," I warned Nyx, not sure whether to be amused or offended by the speed with which he whirled around to face the door.

Apparently, I was doomed to spend my time in Utrea surrounded by beautiful men who either had no interest in me, or were embroiled in circumstances that made dalliances impractical. Or—as presently appeared to be the case with Nyx—both at the same time.

I stripped off the ruined dress, giving it a final, sad look before bundling it up and stuffing it under the bed. Normally, I would hold onto it in hopes that it could either be mended, or the fabric repurposed into something else. Under the circumstances, though, I didn't want to be dragging around anything unnecessary. And besides, both the dress and the slippers stunk like the drainage tunnel.

Of course, so did Nyx. But, hey, at least he was still pretty to look at.

"All done," I told him as I sat on the bed again and slid on my trusty leather boots.

Nyx peered cautiously over his shoulder before turning around. "Cover your hair," he suggested.

"Good idea," I said, and looked for a scarf that would work. No point in making it any easier than necessary for the guards to remember me.

When I was set, I made the rounds of the room, gathering up my meager belongings and stowing them for travel. Lastly, I jammed my hand through a gap in the leather covering of the straw-stuffed mattress and felt around until I found the coin purse I'd hidden there. I'd brought only a small amount of money with me to the palace yesterday, preferring to leave the bulk of the proceeds from selling one of my jewels here.

Nyx's dark brows drew together. "How much money do you *have*, anyway?"

I shrugged. "Just what you saw braided into my hair, plus this." All at once, I realized that I'd dragged Nyx away from his home with only the clothes on his back and a single battered lantern. "Gods. I'm sorry, Nyx—I didn't even think. You left the palace with nothing."

A shadowed look flitted over his face. "It's not as though it's the first time." The words were barely audible.

Somehow, that only made me feel worse. "I have enough money for both of us," I reassured him. "I'll look after you."

His face fascinated me, and I realized that it was because his expression was so mercurial. It shifted back to wry amusement in an instant, though his lips didn't so much as twitch. "Worry about yourself," he told me, not unkindly. "You're the one who just insulted a prince, and I've been taking care of myself for… quite some time."

I wrinkled my nose at him. "The prince insulted me first," I shot back. "Kidnapping me like that—not to mention assuming I was a twenty-two-year-old virgin! I mean, who *does* that?"

Nyx only blinked at me, and I sighed.

"Right, then. I think I've got everything. Let's get out of here." I shot him a sideways glance as I headed for the door. "I don't suppose you know where the Purple Cloak is?"

"Not a clue," he replied.

"Brilliant," I said, and headed into the hallway with a final look over my shoulder.

The candle lit our way back down the cramped stairwell. I blew it out and deposited it on the table with the others. I tossed an extra coin on the worn counter for good measure, hearing the sounds of the proprietor and his staff stirring in the kitchen. No one was in sight, though, and I gestured for Nyx to follow me out into the street. The eastern sky was lightening from navy to cerulean, but the flickering street lamps still lit the roads and plazas around us.

"The early merchants will be out and about by now," Nyx muttered. "I can ask around and get directions from one of them. You should stay back — you're too distinctive, even with that scarf."

I nodded agreement, aware that he was right. The fewer people who noticed me, the safer we'd be. As it was, the guards from earlier might remember me, and the boarding house owner certainly would. It would be best if I didn't leave Oblisii any more of a trail than that.

The market square wasn't far. I hung back in the shadows, watching as Nyx approached first an old woman, and then a middle-aged man, speaking quietly with them. The woman had waved him off, but the man spoke with him for a few moments before turning back to his preparations for the day's business. Nyx hurried back to me.

"It's not far," he said. "Let's move, before it gets too light."

"Sounds good to me," I told him, and followed him toward the opposite end of the square.

There was no telling when my escape from the palace would be discovered. Lesimba and her ilk didn't strike me as the types likely to be early risers, but all it would take was one servant stumbling across my tower of furnishings to raise the alarm.

Nyx led me down a series of turnings, and I was struck once again by the dizzying way in which this city was laid out. I could have wandered all day long and never come across the sprawling two-story building with the purple sign hanging over the door. We paused by mutual accord a short distance away from the inn's entrance. The sun was just beginning to peek through gaps in the buildings, illuminating our surroundings with gold and pink.

"How should we do this?" Nyx asked. "We don't want anyone to notice you, but I'm covered in mud and smell like the sewers."

I thought for a minute. Really, there were only a limited number of options available to us, so I shrugged. "Ignore the mud stains. Act like you own the place. Just stroll in and ask for Aristede."

Nyx gave me the sort of look one gives a person with an obvious mental deficit. I held his gaze, and after a moment he blew out an unhappy breath. "Right," he muttered. "Act like I own the place. Ask for Aristede. Easy."

We crossed the remaining distance to the Purple Cloak and let ourselves inside. I imagined that the bearing of the soldiers sent to slay Utrea's dragons must have been similar to Nyx's bearing as he crossed the threshold of the inn. I stayed a step behind his shoulder, trying to be inconspicuous as we entered the main room. Tables and chairs broke up the large space, with a long counter in front of the far wall, another dark room visible beyond.

No one stood behind the counter at this early hour, and I wondered if we'd have to yell to get someone's attention. Nyx stiffened in front of me. I followed his gaze to see movement in a shadowed part of the room.

A man sat at one of the tables, his chair positioned in the corner, giving him a good view of the rest of the room and the building's entrance. Right now, though, I suspected the only view he was getting was one directed down the cleavage of the serving girl lounging across from him, leaning down on her elbows to flirt—her position giving Nyx and me a first-rate view of her curvy backside.

I started to nudge Nyx to go talk to her, only to grab his shoulder, holding him in place as I registered the white streak running through the man's straight brown hair. A noise somewhere between a groan and a laugh escaped me, followed an instant later by an unexpected flash of irritation at the girl. I quashed it as being both stupid and unworthy. What woman *wouldn't* flirt with Aristede, given the opportunity to do so?

Nyx gave me a flustered look as I threw our hastily conceived plan to the four winds, dragging him behind me as I strode through the warren of furniture and plopped a hip down on the edge of Aristede's table, drawing an outraged squawk from the serving girl. Nyx hung back a few steps, looking like he wanted to sink through the floor.

"Hi," I said, as laughing eyes the color of finely drawn steel landed on me. "Can we come up to your room? I... might have gotten caught up in a *teensy* little problem."

NINE

Aristede lifted an eyebrow, his gray gaze flickering over first me, and then Nyx. He was wearing his long hair tied back in a tight plait at the nape of his neck, the white streak sweeping back from the left side of his forehead. It was a good look on him.

"A problem, my young barbarian friend? Goodness… you *do* shock me." His voice was the smooth drawl I remembered, tinged with teasing and a hint of irony. Honey for the ears.

I resisted the urge to stick my tongue out at him, since that would be undignified. Hey, I was the adopted daughter of a tribal chieftain and a high priest—I was *all about* dignity.

"Then you can be shocked in your room," I told him. "Can we go now, please?"

Aristede gave an easy shrug and aimed a devastating smile at the annoyed serving girl. I realized that she'd probably expected to be the one invited to Aristede's room, and my unworthy little flash of irritation returned.

I quashed it again.

"Forgive me, my dear," he told her, "but it appears I have other business this morning. Perhaps another time. Would you be so good as to send up some bread and cheese for us when the cook gets here?"

I risked a glance at the girl's face. Her mouth was twisted in annoyance, and she made a little *hmph*-ing noise before giving Aristede a tight nod, and me a brief death stare. When she was gone, I turned back to the man in the chair.

"So sorry to interrupt," I said sweetly.

The teasing amusement hadn't left Aristede's face. Neither had the irony. "Think nothing of it. I have the distinct feeling that my morning has just become considerably more interesting."

"Yeah…" I rubbed a hand over the back of my neck. "You don't know the half of it. But that's a conversation for your room—not here. Aristede, this is my new friend Nyx. Nyx, Aristede."

"Hello," Nyx said in that too-soft voice.

Aristede rose and let his gaze play over Nyx more slowly. "A pleasure to meet you, Nyx," he said in a light tone, extending a hand.

Nyx had stepped up to stand at my shoulder after the girl left, but at Aristede's gesture, he… cringed back. There was no other word for it. I frowned, looking up at him and trying to catch his eye, but he wouldn't look at me.

Aristede blinked, and smoothly transformed the gesture of greeting into a sweeping indication toward the staircase along the far wall. "Come with me, both of you," he said pleasantly, his voice giving no indication that Nyx's reaction had bothered him. "The rooms are on the second floor. Breakfast may not be served yet, but I can at least offer you a drink."

I forced a smile and followed him, cataloguing the odd exchange for some future time when things weren't quite so unsettled. Still, I couldn't help noticing the way Nyx followed behind me, using my presence as a buffer between himself and Aristede.

Aristede led us about halfway along the hall to a door on the right and ushered us inside. The room was pleasant; far better appointed than the cheap one I'd rented at the boarding house. He swept in after us, immediately pulling cups from a shelf in the corner and pouring something from a flagon sitting on a small table beside the room's only window.

Nyx was standing stiffly at my shoulder, but Aristede ignored him, handing both cups to me. "There you go. Now, make yourselves comfortable and tell me what trouble you've found."

I handed one of the cups to Nyx and went to sit on one of the two chairs next to the table. I hadn't really appreciated how hungry and thirsty I was until that moment, and I swallowed from the cup appreciatively. It was delicious.

"Mead?" I asked, taking another drink. "Mmm… that's good."

"Nothing but the best at the Purple Cloak," he said, making himself at home on the edge of the large, two-person bed.

Nyx stayed frozen just inside the door, though he did at least drink his mead in slow sips. I resolved to let him be for the time being. After all, he'd just come from a place where his master sometimes beat the stable boys in a drunken rage. Feeling like you were stuck in a situation like that would be enough to make anyone twitchy.

"Is Eldris around?" I asked, not able to tell by looking whether a second person was staying here. Or... a third, for that matter. "And what about Rayth?"

"Neither of them are here at the moment, although Eldris should return later today," Aristede said. "Rayth went ahead to take care of some private business away from the city. I fear we'll be without his particular brand of wit and bonhomie for now."

"Tragic," I said, utterly deadpan.

His mouth twitched at the corner, but his voice remained solemn. "He's not the easiest man to get to know, but you should give him a chance if the opportunity arises."

"I'll take it under consideration," I replied in a dry tone. "But for now, I need your help. I might have to get out of the city, and I don't know who to talk to in order to make that happen. Particularly if I want to avoid a repeat of my last traveling experience."

Aristede huffed a breath of amusement. "Goodness. That certainly didn't take long. Go on... put me out of my misery. Who did you manage to piss off? And how?"

I sighed. "All right. So, I managed to get an audience with the king. He seemed... nice, I guess. If a bit doddering."

Nyx made a faint, choked noise. Possibly he wasn't used to hearing people call the king 'nice.' Or... maybe it was the doddering part? I wasn't sure.

"Go on," Aristede prompted.

"Prince Oblisii was there, too," I continued. "He seemed... less nice. I mean—I'm not completely averse to having someone undress me with his eyes. But there's a creepy way to do it and a not-creepy way to do it, am I right?"

Aristede's steel-gray gaze caressed my curves, making me tingle. Then his eyes met mine again, and he said, "I'd like to think so."

Interestingly, Nyx flushed scarlet. He shifted, his eyes sliding away from mine when I tried to catch them, just as they had after Aristede offered his hand in greeting.

"Anyway," I continued, still watching Nyx from the corner of my eye, "if he'd kept things limited to inappropriate eye-fucking, we could have gone our separate ways afterward and I'd have thought nothing else about it. But, instead, he invited me to stay in the palace. I assumed he meant overnight, since I was supposed to speak further with him about the attack on the road. So I agreed. Because apparently, I'm an idiot."

"You're not an idiot," Aristede said kindly.

"Really? Because I felt like one when he had me locked inside the women's quarters and I discovered from one of the servant girls that I'd just been kidnapped into Prince Creepy-Eye's harem."

Aristede winced.

I barged ahead. "Then, I found out he would be coming back to judge my worthiness based on how much I bled when he screwed me. At which point I decided that escape was... probably a thing I should be doing. So, I climbed out a window and used the roof to get to a different window leading into the kitchens. From there, I found the stables, and that's where I met Nyx. He helped me escape the palace compound through a drainage tunnel. We picked up my belongings from the boarding house I'd been staying at and came straight here."

Our host had listened quietly to my recounting, not offering observations beyond his brief reassurance regarding my mental capacity. Now, though, he rubbed his stubbled chin thoughtfully.

"The old king is hardly a ruler of legend," he mused aloud. "But his son may yet grow into a tyrant."

I watched his face intently. "So, kidnapping women and forcing them to become concubines isn't standard practice in Utrea, then? I'd wondered how he thought he could get away with taking someone he knew had powerful family connections."

"It's not standard practice. As Gladya said, arranged marriages are the norm, at least among the higher classes. Out of curiosity, did you make mention of the fact that you were traveling alone, far from home?"

I thought back, and had to stifle a groan. "The king asked me where my retinue was. I told him I didn't have one, and was only here as a traveler, not an official envoy. Damn it. I basically told Creepy Eyes that I was on my own and there was no one around who would miss me."

Aristede nodded. "Don't beat yourself up. Being a lone traveler visiting the king's court should in no way carry with it the expectation of being abducted into sexual servitude." He sighed. "I'm just glad you were able to get out."

"I've got Nyx to thank for that." I glanced at him, noting that he still looked to be on the verge of flight. "If he hadn't found me and shown me the drainage tunnel, I'd probably still be wandering around, looking for a way out."

"What they did to you wasn't right," he said, his low voice barely more than a whisper.

"Quite so," Aristede agreed. "Unfortunately, I think you're right to worry about what will happen when they discover you've gone missing." He glanced out the window, where the morning sun now illuminated the buildings around us with a fiery glow. "And that will be any time now, I expect."

I nodded. "A couple of guards saw us return to my boarding house this morning. But as far as I know, no one got a good look at us when we came here."

Aristede gave another of those soft, amused huffs. "At least one person did—and I'm afraid you've rather annoyed her."

I frowned, and then realized he was referring to the serving girl whose seduction attempt I'd interrupted downstairs. "Oh. Her. Well, at least my head was covered." I reached up and pulled off the headscarf so I could shake out my hair, my scalp already feeling hot and sweaty beneath it.

Aristede's eyes followed the movement with open appreciation. "Your hair was covered, yes, but those summer-sky eyes of yours are almost as distinctive. Still, I can almost guarantee the guards will waste hours searching inside the palace walls, on the assumption that you couldn't possibly have escaped without being seen. It will take quite a while before they're reduced to sending patrols to search the inns and boarding houses."

I relaxed a fraction, exhaustion sweeping over me without warning. Of course—I'd been up for more than a day straight by this point, and parts of that day had been spent scaling rooftops and slogging through muddy sewage tunnels. I supposed that would exhaust anyone. Maybe I wavered a bit in my chair, because Aristede tilted his head at me.

"Long night," he observed, his gaze moving to briefly encompass Nyx as well. "For both of you, I'll wager. Why don't you get a few hours of sleep?"

A knock on the door interrupted our quiet conversation, making Nyx jump. He sidled away as Aristede opened it and accepted the tray of food from a boy no older than ten. He rummaged at his belt for a moment and came up with a copper coin, which he flipped into the child's waiting hand. The small face lit up.

"Thank you, sir!" he squeaked.

"You're welcome," Aristede told him solemnly. "Come up and tell me if anyone starts asking around about a woman with golden hair, and there will be another one waiting for you."

"Yes, sir!" the child piped. "I'll come and tell you right away!"

I smiled, once the boy was gone and the door locked behind him. "Have you been hiding a devious streak, Aristede?" I teased.

He handed me a chunk of warm bread and some cheese, raising his eyebrow at me as he did. "Who said I'm hiding it?"

I laughed. Nyx cautiously accepted a portion of the food as well, and Aristede settled into the chair across from me to eat his own breakfast.

"As I was saying," he continued, "if you two would like to rest for a few hours, I'll head out and see what gossip is making the rounds. It will give us a better feel for how much effort the prince is likely to expend on trying to find you."

"Hopefully he'll cut his losses once he finds out I've left the palace grounds," I muttered around a mouthful of bread.

Nyx had apparently inhaled his food already, because he brushed crumbs from his hands, still not meeting my eyes as he spoke. "You pricked his pride. Powerful men don't take kindly to that."

"True words," Aristede agreed grimly. "Still, we can hope." He, too, finished the last of his meal, and stood. "Lock the door behind me. Don't open it unless you hear three short knocks, followed by two long, and another three short. That will either be me or Eldris. For anyone else, have your friend Nyx speak to them through the door and send them away."

"All right," I said, hoping that nothing would disturb us for a few hours so I could get some rest.

Aristede peered out the window. "It's not ideal, but in case of emergency, you can generally jump down from a second story window without injury if you hang by your fingertips first. If it comes to that, I'll look for you in the alleys behind the abattoir. That's an unpleasant enough area that the guards tend to avoid it."

"Had a lot of experience jumping from second story windows, have you?" I couldn't help asking.

"A gentleman never tells," he replied.

I snorted. "Fine. Got it. And Aristede… thank you."

Aristede smiled and brushed his knuckles along my cheek. The touch was so light it was barely there, but I had to suppress a shiver of reaction, and my eyes slipped closed of their own accord. This man should come with some kind of warning, like a red ribbon braided into a horse's tail to tell other riders that it kicks.

"As I said," he drawled in that honey-laced voice, "my morning just got considerably more interesting. That's a good thing… I don't do well with boredom. Sleep well, Frella. I don't expect you'll be disturbed this morning."

He gathered up his weapons belt and sent a friendly nod in Nyx's direction before letting himself out of the room. Nyx hesitated for a moment before crossing to the door and locking it behind him.

"Frella," he echoed, not turning around to look at me. "Is that your name?"

I blinked. Hadn't I told him? Thinking back, I realized that I hadn't. Clearly, desperate nighttime escapes played havoc with what few manners I possessed in the normal course of things.

"That's me," I said lightly. "And it's a pleasure to make your acquaintance properly. Now, I'm getting some sleep. This bed is huge, so you're welcome to join me."

"That's... not..." Nyx stuttered, but I cut him off.

"Your virtue is safe with me, Nyx. Promise. I can barely keep my eyes open; I don't really have the energy to ravish you." I frowned. "Though I can't guarantee I won't snore. I never have figured out for certain if my brother was just teasing me when he told me that, or if he was serious."

The mattress was beckoning—covers neatly made and pillows fluffed. I wondered if Aristede was a habitually early riser, remembering that he'd taken the last watch the night we camped by the dry riverbed.

It bothered me a bit to stick my dirty boots under the sheets, but under the circumstances, practicality demanded it. I refused to be stuck hopping around on one foot trying to get them back on if we ended up having to make a run for it. Leaving Nyx to wrestle with whatever misgivings kept him frozen across the room, I made myself comfortable next to the wall, turning my back to the room and leaving a large, unclaimed space behind me in case Nyx changed his mind at some point.

The bed was really, *really* comfortable. It took almost no time at all before I drifted off, waking only momentarily some time later as a weight settled on the other side of the mattress, shifting around a bit before growing still.

I smiled at the wall, not turning to look, and was asleep again a few moments later.

TEN

A pattern of knocks roused me from heavy sleep some unknown amount of time later. Three short, two long, three short. Nyx jolted upright next to me, but didn't rise to open the door. I blinked the blurriness from my eyes and shuffled to the foot of the bed so I could get up without having to crawl over him.

"Coming!" I called, the abrupt awakening making me uncoordinated as I stumbled across the room. I threw back the metal latch and swung the door open to reveal a tall, broad form that nearly took up the whole doorway.

"Frella?" Eldris asked, surprise in his tone.

I grinned and threw my arms around him. "Eldris!"

It was, perhaps, an overly effusive greeting for someone I'd only known for a day or so, but Eldris merely chuckled and hugged me back, walking us backward a few steps so he could shut the door behind him. I freed myself, still smiling as I shoved the disastrous tangle of my hair away from my face.

"Hi," I said, a bit sheepishly. "I came back. Still want to teach me those self defense moves?"

He laughed aloud at that, a booming noise that made something twist pleasantly in my chest. "I'd love to, sweet thing," he said, before his eyes moved over my shoulder to Nyx. "Now, who's this, then?"

I followed his gaze, expecting to see Nyx frozen with fear in the presence of the massive, dark-skinned Kulawi warrior. To my surprise, though, he looked wary but not paralyzed.

"I'm Nyx," he said in that quiet voice. "I'm... with her."

"Yes, he's with me," I confirmed. "I... kind of sort of got kidnapped into Prince Oblisii's harem after a royal audience with him, and Nyx helped me escape from the palace."

Eldris stared at me for a beat. "You're a trouble magnet, you are," he said. "Should've put a bell on you when I had the chance."

I flushed a bit and cleared my throat.

"Where'd Ari get to, anyway?" Eldris asked.

"I gather he's out plying the local gossipmongers, trying to find out whether Oblisii's coming after me or not."

Eldris nodded. "Makes sense." He shot a wry smile at Nyx, who still hadn't moved from his perch on the edge of the bed. "Thanks for bringin' our girl here back to us, mate."

"It was more a case of her bringing me," Nyx said under his breath, and Eldris snorted.

"That works, too," he said, and stretched, shoulders popping. "Any of that mead left?"

"A bit," I told him, "and some bread from this morning."

He helped himself and flopped into a chair. It creaked a bit under his powerful frame. Even seated, he didn't have to lift his gaze very far to meet mine, his eyebrows quirking. "Right, Trouble Girl. While we're waiting for Ari to get back, I want to hear this story from the beginning."

⌒⟡⌒

When I finished recounting the story a second time, Eldris shook his head at me. "Good goddess, woman."

I pursed my lips. "I can't help it if the prince of Utrea is a lecherous creep. All I did was tell him that there are bandits on the trade road with his mark on their saddle blankets."

Eldris sobered. "Wasn't trying to blame you, sweet thing." He sighed, long and low. His next words were almost as soft as Nyx's murmured speech. "Sometimes I hate this place."

"What do you mean?" I asked.

He tried to smile, but it didn't reach his eyes. "People acting like they can own other people. 'S not right."

Nyx shifted on the bed.

I nodded. "My brother and his bondmates fought a war on Eburos to free all the slaves. What Oblisii is doing isn't quite the same, but in the end it's just as bad."

"He's going to come after you," Nyx said. "You mustn't let him take you back."

I raised an eyebrow. "I've no intention of letting him take me back. As soon as Aristede gets here, I'll figure out where to go next. I'd hoped to spend more time in Safaad, but there's nothing tying me here."

Eldris gave me a cheeky wink, his brief black mood giving way to what I suspected was a naturally happy temperament. "Aww, now you're just hurting my feelings, Frella."

And… it was true. I might have meant the words as I said them, but I would be sad to say goodbye to Eldris and Aristede. I wondered if Nyx, at least, would want to come with me? I hoped so.

The smile I mustered for Eldris felt a bit wistful despite my best efforts. "Everyone leaves sooner or later, big man. That's just life."

If I'd learned one lesson in my twenty-two years, it was that.

"I hope that's not the case," Eldris said mildly. "There are some people I'd be loath to give up."

This was a subject I found more than a bit uncomfortable, so I let it slide. Eldris cocked his head, and the faint sounds of footsteps in the hall reached my ears a moment later.

"Sounds like Ari's back," he said, and rose to open the door without waiting for the prearranged series of knocks.

Indeed, Aristede entered, sparing Eldris a smile and a tip of the chin as he passed.

"How did you know it was him?" I asked, my brow furrowing.

Eldris shrugged a brawny shoulder. "Spend a few years with someone, and you start to recognize their tread. Also, the dagger loop on that damned weapons belt is too close to his sword hilt. It makes noise when he walks."

Aristede unbuckled the belt in question and set it aside, throwing Eldris a smirk as the larger man returned to his chair. "At least it saves me having to knock when you're around," he said.

He tossed me something wrapped in cloth and I caught it out of reflex.

"Food," he said by way of explanation.

I unwrapped the round of dark, grainy flatbread and went to perch next to Nyx—pleased when he didn't cringe away. I tore off a quarter of the loaf for him and a quarter for myself before tossing what was left back to Aristede.

"Thanks," I told him. "So, what's the news? Anything?"

Aristede put the bread on the table and wandered around to stand behind Eldris' chair, leaning his forearms casually on the high back. "Palace guards have been out in force this afternoon, I'm sorry to say. They haven't been giving out details, but it's fairly obvious they're searching for someone."

I sighed. "I suppose it was inevitable. I guess he doesn't want to advertise that he lost a concubine."

Aristede tipped his head in agreement. "I expect not. At any rate, the guards will show up here at some point. There are only so many inns and rooming houses to search."

He was right, of course. "I guess I'll need to find some transportation out of the city. Can you help with that?"

He nodded, not moving from his slouch against the back of Eldris' chair. "Probably. Though it depends very much on where you intend to go."

I thought about it for a bit. "Kulawi," I decided. "It sounds like a much nicer place than Utrea."

Eldris seemed to be looking very intently at me. "You think so? It's a long way from here, you know."

I stared right back at him. "And... your point is what, exactly?"

"I'm just sayin'."

Nyx had gone very quiet again since Aristede's return, but I turned to him. "What about it? Any interest in seeing what lies across the Great Southern Desert?"

He blinked, as though the question had taken him by surprise. "I... don't know."

It occurred to me that while there might not be anything holding *me* here, that didn't mean Nyx didn't have ties to Safaad that would make him want to stay.

"Do you have family here?" I asked, more gently.

But he shook his head. "No. I'm not from here."

The conversation was interrupted by a flurry of knocks at the door. I tensed, but it certainly wasn't the sort of knocking you'd expect from a serious-faced guard. More what you'd expect from —

"The boy," Aristede said.

"What boy?" Eldris asked.

"Our hastily acquired lookout," Aristede explained. "I told him to come back if anyone from the palace started snooping around."

"From the sound of it, any guard worth their salt will have noticed him rushing up here and followed him right to our door," Eldris grumbled.

"Yes, well," Aristede sighed. "You two—under the bed. Don't make a sound, and leave this to me. Eldris, deal us some cards."

"Yeah, yeah. I know the drill," Eldris said, pulling out a deck of playing cards and dealing them out on the table.

I stared between them, Nyx frozen beside me. "Wait, what?" I asked.

"Coming," Aristede called to the frantically knocking boy, lowering his voice to hiss. "Under. The bed. *Now.*"

Somewhat to my surprise, Nyx grabbed my arm and more or less dragged me down to the floor. I eyed the space under the bed. A heartbeat later, a surprisingly strong grip had me on my back, staring at the leather straps holding up the mattress less than a hand's breadth above my nose. The bed was definitely more comfortable when you came at it from the other direction.

Nyx and I shuffled as far underneath it as we could get, until he was right up against the wall and I was pressed next to him, shoulder to shoulder. I held my breath as the door opened.

"I, uh, brought you some more mead," said the child from earlier. His voice was breathless and high-pitched—the exact opposite of casual.

"And it's about time, too," Aristede said sharply, and I had to appreciate his quick thinking in providing a reason to any listening ears for why the boy might be in such a hurry.

"Stop snapping at the boy," Eldris said patiently, as though he didn't have a care in the world. "Give 'im a copper and send 'im on his way. I'm winning this hand."

"Yes, fine," Aristede sighed. "Oh—hallo there. Can I help you gents?"

"King's guard," said a deep, no-nonsense voice.

I froze, breathing shallowly, aware of Nyx trembling where his arm pressed against mine.

"Indeed?" Aristede said. "Come in, come in—both of you. What can we do for you today?"

I had to press my lips together to hold in an outraged squeak. He was *inviting them in*? I altered my opinion of Aristede from dangerously attractive to dangerously *insane*. Beside me, Nyx's shaking grew more pronounced. I wondered if he was claustrophobic, or just worried about getting caught. Without thought, I brushed my fingers against his and tangled our hands together. A moment later, he squeezed back hard.

His trembling grew less noticeable, though.

"We're searching for a woman," one of the guards was saying.

Eldris grunted. "Yeah? Well, if you find her, send her our way. It's been a while."

Someone snorted, though I couldn't tell whether it Aristede or one of the guards. My vantage point meant that all I could see was boots, and craning my neck to see even that much tugged painfully on a hank of hair trapped under my back. I held onto Nyx's hand and tried to tell myself that the dust we'd disturbed wasn't making me want to sneeze. The careful way Nyx was breathing through his shakes made me suspect he was telling himself the same thing.

"As you can see, we're sadly lacking in women at the moment," Aristede said. "Anything distinguishing about her? We can keep an eye out. Especially if there's a reward involved?" His voice trailed off hopefully.

"No reward," snapped the first guard, who seemed to have a stick lodged more firmly up his ass than the second one who'd spoken. "She's a foreigner. Pale skinned, with blue eyes and golden hair."

"Golden hair?" Aristede mused thoughtfully. "Well, at least she ought to be easy to find. I'd remember something like that, I expect."

"I should say so," Eldris agreed.

"Interesting," said the no-nonsense guard, "since one of the wenches here told us that a woman of that description followed the guest with a white streak in his hair upstairs to his room this morning."

My heart lurched and started tripping frantically. *Damn it.* I'd always hated it when women tried to visit petty revenge on other women they considered competition. I hated it even more now that I was the target and the revenge was far more than petty.

Aristede only laughed, even as Eldris said, "What the fuck? You brought a woman up here and didn't even wait for me to get back? Selfish twat. I'll do more than take your damned money at cards!"

"I would have waited," Aristede defended. "Don't glare at me like that, you great oaf—I *would* have! Look, you two... that's not exactly what happened. This serving girl. Is she buxom, with a slight gap between her front teeth?"

"Yes, that's right," said the second guard.

"Ah. I imagine she's a bit cross with me, and thought she could stir up trouble." Aristede sighed audibly. "In fact, *she* was the one I brought up here. Only to discover after a few minutes of play that, while she seems an open-minded and fun-loving girl, she also has a case of the pox bad enough to fell a horse. I'm afraid I bundled her out of the room as soon as I laid eyes on all the, uh... all of the weeping sores. I'm sure you understand."

From his tone, he might've been confessing to a priest at the temple rather than lying through his teeth to a palace guardsman. I changed my estimation from *dangerously insane* to just plain *dangerous*.

The second guard—at least, I assumed it was him—stifled a chuckle. Badly.

"Feel free to take a look around," Aristede went on. "Can I offer either of you a drink, now that the boy finally got around to delivering it?"

"Oh get over yourself, you posh bastard," Eldris grumbled. "They don't wanna stop for a drink when they're working. And you're just trying to put off the inevitable thrashing at cards that I'm about to dish out."

"No need to rub it in," Aristede muttered. "That's almost a week's earnings on the line, you know."

"Come on," said the guard with the stick up his ass. "We've wasted enough time here."

"You're certain you won't stay for a drink?" Aristede asked, the words accompanied by the sound of the door opening. "No? The mead is quite good…"

The door closed.

"Ah well. Back to our foolish gambling it is, then."

"Too right," Eldris agreed.

Once a few moments of silence confirmed that the guards were gone, I let Nyx go and scooted quietly out from under the bed. Nyx followed a bit less quietly, and with a bit more desperation. So—claustrophobia after all, apparently.

Aristede held up an imperious hand, commanding silence for several more moments. I held my breath, listening, but I couldn't even hear the guards' footsteps anymore.

"Relax," Eldris said in a normal voice. "They're gone."

Aristede lowered his hand, and I let the air out of my lungs.

"Agreed," he said.

I glared up at Aristede, knowing I probably resembled nothing so much as a dust mop at this point. "You are as mad as a drunken hare in a dog kennel," I accused. "What the hell were you *thinking*?"

Eldris laughed, a low, masculine sound that came dangerously close to distracting me from my incredulity.

Aristede only shrugged. "What? The ruse worked, didn't it?"

I continued to glare at him. "You're also way too practiced with that whole, 'Quick, under the bed!' routine. Just saying."

"Yeah... he's had extensive practice hiding people in his bedroom who weren't supposed to be there," Eldris said.

There was an edge to his tone that I couldn't decipher, but I was still hung up on my exasperation with Aristede. "In what world is that something you *practice*?"

Aristede only raised one gracefully swept eyebrow at me. "I wouldn't call it *practice* so much as real world experience. After all, you're here in my bedroom when you're not supposed to be, aren't you?"

Eldris made another noise I couldn't parse, but Nyx interrupted the pointless exchange. "What do we do now? We can't wait around for days to organize transportation out of the city."

I tried to tell myself that a single close call with guards didn't mean I'd be relentlessly hounded. Not as long as I didn't go out in daylight, anyway—because no doubt word of the golden-haired girl wanted by the guards was spreading like wildfire around the city.

"We could take 'em up to the cave," Eldris said. "They'd be safe there."

Aristede looked at him so sharply that it took me by surprise. His whole demeanor changed in a heartbeat, from smooth and playful to cold and distant.

"No," he said.

ELEVEN

"What cave?" I asked. "What are you two talking about?"

Eldris' eyes flickered to mine briefly before he focused on Aristede again. "You know we'll have to do something eventually, Ari. Maybe these two stumbled back here for a reason."

"*Ahem.*" I cleared my throat meaningfully.

"And *you* know the risks," Aristede retorted, paying me no mind. "You want to bank on some nebulous concept of *fate*, Riss? *Really?*"

I dragged my dust-coated self up from the floor and pushed between them, grabbing Aristede's loose tunic-front in my fist. "I don't appreciate being talked around any more than I appreciate being abducted into a harem. Now. *What. Are. You. Talking. About.*"

Steel-gray eyes landed on me heavily. I won't lie—I was finding this sudden facet of coldness in him disconcerting.

"My associate is suggesting something dangerous for everyone involved," he said, and I wondered when Eldris had gone from someone whose chair-back he leaned casually against to an *associate*. "You'll have to forgive my lapse in manners, but for now, this is between the two of us."

I frowned, but released his clothing.

"We could sneak them out on horseback tonight, riding double along the riverbed," Eldris said. "We'd have to rest the horses more often, but we could be there in a little more than a day."

I backed off a step so I could watch them both.

"And if the you-know-what showed up?" Aristede shot back. "What then?"

"Then there would be five of us rather than three," Eldris replied evenly. "Like I said, you know we'll have to do something sooner or later."

Aristede stared at him unflinchingly for so long that the air in the room started to turn heavy. Eldris didn't move or break gaze, even though it was all I could do not to start jumping up and down, demanding answers. Good gods, much longer and all four of us would drown in the stifling atmosphere.

"Fine," Aristede said eventually, still not giving any ground with his cold eyes. "But I leave it to you to explain the decision to Rayth."

Eldris only shrugged. "Rayth is his own worst enemy. You know that as well as I do."

"I fear that can be said of everyone here, my friend," said Aristede, his manner finally softening to something more like what I was used to.

I eyed them warily. "So you propose to take Nyx and me to a cave where Rayth is staying? Why is Rayth staying in a cave?"

"To avoid prying eyes," Aristede said unhelpfully.

"It's remote, and it's private," Eldris said. "Seems like just the thing while we figure out what to do next, Trouble."

I frowned at him, though I couldn't exactly dispute it. "All right. So, where is this place? In the mountains somewhere?"

"Yes," Aristede said. "It's difficult to get to. Most wouldn't bother to try. But there's a spring-fed lake nearby, foraging to be had— even game to hunt."

"And Rayth is there, instead of staying here at a nice inn? Does the spring run with wine instead of water?" I couldn't help asking.

"You should give Rayth more of a chance," Eldris said. "Just because he bested you in a sparring match—"

I felt my cheeks flush at the reminder. "That's got nothing to do with it," I lied.

"Mmm," Aristede hummed, and shot another look at Eldris. "You understand my reluctance, here?"

"Pfft. They'll get used to each other."

I was on the fence about needing to get used to Rayth, but this was still the best offer I was likely to get. I shifted my focus to Nyx, who was still sitting on the floor next to the bed. "What about it? Want to come with us and share a cave in the mountains with an infuriating, angry drunkard?"

Never let it be said that I couldn't sell an idea to someone.

Nyx let his shoulders lift and lower. "I lived up there for a little over a year after—" He cut himself off. "Well… it was a time when I didn't really have anyplace else to go, that's all. It's not too bad if you know how to trap game and which plants are safe to eat. It won't even be cold at this time of year."

I turned back to the other two. "In that case, I guess we're going to visit Rayth. You want to leave tonight?"

"Yeah," Eldris said, "That'd be for the best. The longer you're here in Safaad, the more chance someone'll see you and tell the wrong person."

Aristede seemed resigned to the new plan, if not precisely happy. "You should both get some more rest while you have the chance. It will be a difficult journey."

"You and Eldris should rest, too," I pointed out. "I already got a shot at the bed today. Lend me a bedroll and I'll be fine on the floor. Nyx and I even dusted it earlier."

Aristede shook his head. "Don't be daft, Frella." He eyed the generously sized mattress. "That will fit three, if you're not bothered by sharing with Nyx and Eldris. I don't sleep all that much anyway."

"You should try to grab a nap, at least," Eldris said. "Fording the river bend is tricky at the best of times, never mind in the dark. Don't want to be falling asleep at an inopportune moment."

"I will," Aristede promised, "but there's no point in me tossing and turning in bed, keeping everybody else awake. Eldris, would you mind fetching up a ewer of water for the washbasin before we retire? Since one of the serving girls is after me."

Eldris huffed, but rose and headed for the door. "With the trail of serving girls you've left behind, mate, it's a miracle there are any inns left at all where you can show your face."

"I'm certain I have no idea what you mean," Aristede said blandly.

Eldris returned a few minutes later with water, and the four of us freshened up before extinguishing the candles. I claimed the middle of the bed, with Eldris jammed against the wall and Nyx closest to the edge. It wasn't an unpleasant place to be, I decided, with a big grumbly bear on my left and a shy, beautiful stag on my right.

With my eyes closed, I heard Aristede shuffling around for a moment before the chair by the window creaked, and I took a moment to wonder what troubled his dreams so badly. Before long, though, I was asleep—my previous slumber evidently not enough to overcome the exhaustion of the last couple of days.

It seemed like barely any time had passed at all when a noise woke me. I blinked, the room coming into focus as silver moonlight streamed through the window. Nyx was no longer lying next to me, but rather sitting on the edge of the bed, elbows resting on knees, watching the figure slumped in a chair across the room.

Aristede must have drifted off with his head on his arms, upper body resting on the table. Now, though, he was twitching restlessly, low sounds like a child's moan of fear emerging, half-muffled, from his lips. I'd seen enough night terrors to recognize one, and I experienced a flash of irritation that Nyx was just sitting there, watching it like some sort of a show.

I swung into a sitting position, trying not to jostle Eldris awake, and scooted around Nyx's body until I could get to my feet. A hand closed around my wrist, halting me before I could take a single step. I whirled on Nyx, whose green-ringed eyes moved to meet mine in the weak light.

"Don't," he said, barely more than the shape of a word. "Never wake a dreaming soldier."

I drew breath, but without knowing what words I wanted to say, it stayed in my lungs, trapped. Before I could untangle my tongue, a larger, darker form brushed past, Eldris moving almost silently despite his bulk.

"What a load of rot," he muttered. "Always wake a dreaming soldier. Just be ready to duck when you do."

I subsided in Nyx's grip, and his fingers slid away from my wrist.

"Ari," Eldris said, and grasped his shoulder in one hand. "C'mon. Get your head out of the past."

I caught my breath as Aristede snarled and came up swinging. Eldris blocked the first blow with a forearm and darted his head back, quick as a snake, to avoid the second. Aristede nearly fell out of the chair when his fist met no resistance, and Eldris steadied him with a hand splayed across his chest, over his heart.

"Wha—?" Aristede croaked, his voice hoarse as though he'd been screaming. Maybe in his head, he had been. He blinked owlishly in the moonlight. "Oh. Sorry. I woke you again."

"You woke all of us, mate, but don't worry about it. We should probably get going anyway." Eldris let him go with a final pat to the chest, and Aristede scrubbed a hand over his face, running his fingers through the smooth length of his hair. My fingers itched to do the same, brushing it back from his pale features.

I shook my head, trying to wake up the rest of the way. There was far more to the man slouched in the chair than the silver-tongued temptation I'd originally assumed him to be. How much of him was that, how much was the cold, calculating logician I'd seen the previous evening, and how much was the desperate dreamer fighting for his life as he awoke remained to be seen. But if there was a single word I could use to describe what I'd seen of Aristede so far, it was *complicated*.

"Are we leaving, then?" I asked in lieu of any comment on what had just happened.

Aristede's jaw cracked in a yawn. "Yes," he said. "Might as well."

"You go get the horses saddled and bring them around back," Eldris said, stretching until his spine cracked. "Probably for the best if these two leave by the window. I can lower them down and then leave the regular way."

Aristede nodded, gathering up his weapons belt and a pair of saddlebags as he left without a word. I'd slept in my boots again, but I strapped on my throwing knives and splashed water from the basin on my face. That didn't stop me from feeling like I was stumbling around in a daze, but if Eldris was serious about lowering us through the window, I suspected that would wake me up in a hurry.

Figuring that it might come in handy, I refilled Nyx's stolen lantern with oil from one of the lamps and handed it to him, along with one of my six daggers. He stared at the blade in his palm for a long moment as though unsure what to do with it, but then he stuck it in his boot.

It wasn't all that long before a soft whistle like a birdcall drifted through the window.

"Ready?" Eldris asked.

"To be lowered through a window?" I asked. "How would you like me to answer that?"

White teeth flashed in the dark. "I can send down the packs and bedrolls first. We'll see how they fare."

"Ha," I told him, not amused.

"I'll go first," Nyx said in his soft voice. "I can catch you at the bottom."

That actually did make me feel a bit better, and I tried to smile at him. His eyes had already slid away, though. He was awfully good at making me forget he was there, and I resolved not to let him use that trick on me so often. "Thanks," I said, taking a chance and brushing his jaw with my fingers, guiding his gaze back up to mine.

Though his expression was uncertain, he didn't flinch away. I gave him the smile I'd tried to convey earlier. His mouth moved as though he might have been trying to smile back, but had forgotten how. I wished for more light in the room.

Eldris was already tossing the packs and bedrolls down to Aristede. When he was done, he turned to us. "C'mon then. Let's get a shift on."

Nyx took a deep breath and crossed the room, lifting his legs through the window with a strength and grace I wouldn't have expected from someone so uncomfortable in his own skin. He twisted on the sill and grasped wrists with Eldris, who barely seemed to strain as he lowered the smaller man down as far as he could reach.

"Three… two… one… and down you go," he said, and I heard feet hitting gravel a moment later.

"Is he all right?" I asked, crowding forward to peer at the ground below. Nyx waved up, unhurt.

"Have a bit of faith, Trouble," Eldris chided, and nudged me with an elbow.

I let him support me as I scooted into position, wondering if he could hear the nervous galloping of my heart. The darkness, while far from complete, made it difficult to judge distances, and anytime I peered down from a height, my mind tried to recall the feeling of losing my footing on loose shale and tumbling down the rocky cliff face in the forests outside of Draebard when I was ten.

Eldris' grip was firm and reassuring, though. Rather than look down, I focused on his face as I walked my feet down the outer wall. As he had done with Nyx, he lowered me effortlessly until his head and shoulders were outside the window, his arms and mine stretched out straight.

"I've got you," said a quiet voice from not very far below me.

"You'll be all right, sweet thing," Eldris assured. "Get ready in three… two… one… and go."

It was all I could do to pry my fingers from his wrists at the same moment he let go. I pushed away from the wall with my feet and focused on staying upright, not locking my knees. A decidedly girly squeak made it past my lips despite my best efforts, but then hands were closing around my waist, softening the impact of my boots with the ground.

"Well done," Aristede murmured from nearby.

The hands let go of me, and fortunately my shaky legs took my weight without buckling.

"Let's not do that again. *Ever*," I said, glad my voice didn't tremble.

"Those are the words of someone who needs more practice," Aristede teased.

I glared at him. "Those are the words of someone who has a totally valid reason for *not liking heights*," I shot back.

"How do you want to do this?" Nyx asked before the sniping could continue further. "You and I together are probably about the same weight as Eldris and Frella together, but his horse is more powerful than yours."

"We'll need to rotate between walking and riding," Aristede said. "But the animals should be able to handle all four of us long enough to at least get out of the city. The faster we do that, the better."

"Agreed," Nyx said, though he looked uncomfortable—his shoulders stiff in the moonlight.

I remembered the way he'd cringed back from Aristede's extended hand upon their first meeting, and the careful way Aristede had avoided getting too close to him since then.

"Is riding double with someone going to be a problem for you?" I asked Nyx, deciding to take the bull by the horns.

There was a beat of silence. "Is there a choice?" Nyx asked.

Aristede regarded him steadily. "Not really." He seemed to weigh his words for a moment before continuing. "Whoever it was, though... in your past, I mean—I'm not him."

"I know that," Nyx snapped in the closest thing to anger I'd heard from him.

"I know you know. Do you have a weapon?"

I thought of the knife I'd handed Nyx, now stowed in his boot.

"Yes," he said. "A blade."

Aristede nodded. "Then you'll ride behind me with your dagger within easy reach. You saw my ghosts earlier. For reasons I'm not inclined to discuss, I don't like the idea of having an armed stranger at my back. We can be equally uncomfortable. Fair?"

Nyx mulled over his words. "Fair."

Aristede's bay mare snorted and tossed her head while I was still trying to unpick the threads of that short exchange. Eldris appeared around the corner a moment later.

"We ready?" he asked.

"I think so," I replied.

Aristede had already stowed our gear on the horses. He swung onto his mare with an easy motion, and held her still while Nyx accepted a leg up from Eldris. Once they were settled, Eldris took up the reins of his chestnut gelding and mounted.

Obviously remembering the trip to Safaad, he reached a hand down to me and grinned.

"Any excuse to get you cozied up to me, sweet thing," he quipped.

I grinned back and took the proffered hand, swinging up behind him. I had to grab his jerkin with my free hand to drag myself into place on the tall, stocky animal, but Eldris was immovable in his easy strength and bulk. He didn't so much as shift as I used him as a climbing trellis, settling my rump behind the cantle of the saddle.

When I was situated, I wrapped my arms around his torso. "Sure you want to keep trouble this close?" I teased.

I couldn't see it, but I could hear the grin in his voice as he replied, "Oh, trust me. I wouldn't have it any other way."

We headed out, a silent caravan of two, keeping to backstreets and alleys. The city was such a maze, it was amazing to me that anyone could find their way around in daylight, much less at night. The roads we were following weren't lit with the street lamps that seemed ubiquitous in the more traveled areas. No doubt that was part of the reason Aristede and Eldris were using them.

The horses' hooves sounded loud on the cobbles, but aside from a couple of instances when our two guides rode into the deeper shadows and halted the animals while the glow of a lantern—presumably carried by guards—moved past, we didn't see anyone. Whatever else could be said about it, Safaad didn't seem to be a city with much in the way of nightlife. This was in stark contrast to

Rhyth, where my brother lived. There, it seemed like the city woke up when the sun went down. Here, the atmosphere of sleepy indifference was almost palpable as we made our way to the outskirts.

As with every city of a certain size that I'd ever come across, Safaad had a river. When we came to it, we left the roadways completely in favor of scooting down the steep bank. I gathered that it flowed down directly from the mountains, so even in summer it was still running strong. We splashed through the shallows, following it upstream.

Safaad fell away behind us, and the banks turned rocky and sheer. The moon illuminated a bend in the watercourse. We had been largely silent, even though there was no particular reason to remain that way now that we were out of the city. I felt Eldris draw in a deep breath and let it out as he reined his horse to a halt on a small, sandy jut of land at the base of the rock walls.

"I hate this part," he said conversationally as Aristede and Nyx arrived next to us.

"We all hate this part," Aristede agreed, and nudged Nyx. "Down you get. You, too, Frella."

TWELVE

All four of us dismounted, crowded together on the cramped sandbar. I eyed the river course ahead of us, with its steep, unscalable walls. "Does that mean what I think it means?" I asked.

"We'll have to swim it," Eldris confirmed. "It's not as bad in summer as it would be in the springtime. That's just fucking dangerous. Let's get everything that won't stand getting wet off the horses, and get this over with."

"You don't want to wait until morning?" Nyx asked uncertainly.

"Not so you'd notice," Aristede replied. "We're not *that* far from the city yet."

I sighed, leaning down to pull off my boots and stockings. I'd done this sort of thing on a handful of occasions over the course of my life. At least it wasn't cold tonight.

"Hand me a pair of saddlebags," I said, figuring I could stick my boots inside and balance them on my head to keep the contents dry.

Eldris balked. "You don't need to do that, sweet thing. The three of us can carry our stuff."

I turned to him and gripped my breasts, lifting them until they pointed in the general direction of his face. "Don't be stupid. You've seen these already, right? Well, guess what? *They float.*"

A choked laugh came from behind me—Aristede, at a guess. Eldris shook his head at me, but a smile twitched his lips.

"Seriously," I went on, "I'm a good swimmer. We can each hold onto one side of a horse. It'll be fine. You just have to keep your legs out of the way of *their* legs."

Aristede handed me his saddlebags, and I jammed my boots and stockings in the already tightly packed space. The others grabbed the remaining pair of saddlebags and the two bedrolls, readying themselves. Not surprisingly, the horses weren't too keen on the plan. Eldris gave Aristede's mare a smart slap on the rump with the end of his reins when she balked, and the startled animal plunged forward into the water.

His gelding followed more readily, and I stayed even with the horse's left shoulder, while Eldris stayed on the right. The bottom dropped away quickly, and soon we were swimming. Not surprisingly, the horses wanted to turn around and head back downstream, and we had to keep shooing them in the direction we wanted to go.

Also, while the current wasn't dangerously fast, making headway against it was a challenge. It was clear that Aristede and Eldris were angling across the waterway toward the far bank to try and minimize this, but the far bank felt like it kept getting farther away, since we were negotiating a bend in the river at the same time. We couldn't rely on the horses to tow us along, or they wouldn't have been able to make progress at all against the flow. So we kicked and paddled, while also trying to keep the burdens balanced on our heads dry.

All in all, it wasn't the most fun I'd ever had.

By the time our feet touched the steep bank on the far side, I was shaky enough from the exertion that I came perilously close to getting tangled up with Eldris' plunging horse — and we still couldn't get out of the water completely. Even here on the far side, the rock wall came right down to the river's edge.

Eldris and Aristede got the animals stopped, standing stiff-legged but calm on the sloping bottom. I was on the lower side of the slope, trying to keep my balance on the shifting gravel with the river lapping at my chin.

"Let the horses blow for a few minutes and we'll make the final push for the trail leading out of the canyon," Aristede said, coughing a bit. From the sound of his voice, he'd taken on a bit of water at some point.

Eldris snaked an arm under his horse's neck and snagged me. "Get on the high side, short stuff. You're making me nervous down there."

I scrambled toward him, trying not to smack the poor gelding in the face with the saddlebags as I switched sides. The horse shook its head in agitation and sneezed, blowing snot all over me.

"How much further?" I asked through gritted teeth, after I'd found a relatively stable spot to stand on that put the waterline a few inches above my waist.

"About a quarter league's travel until we can get away from the river," Eldris said. "Last time we came through here, there were a couple of spots where we had to swim again and a few where there's enough of a bank to get out of the water completely. It changes all the time, though."

"It's a tricky area to negotiate," Aristede said, sounding more himself now. "But, that means most people don't try, which is to our advantage. The terrain at the top of the cliffs is all bare rock and boulders, crisscrossed with gullies and crevasses that a horse could easily fall into—especially at night."

I shuddered, unexpectedly blindsided by early childhood memories of my father's death in just such a crevasse. He'd been traveling in winter during a snowstorm, and had blindly fallen into a deep ravine in the rocks. He'd died instantly, and his companions hadn't been able to retrieve his body until the following spring.

By that time, all they'd been able to bring back to my brother and me was a bundle of gnawed bones. That had been my second lesson in the inevitability of loved ones leaving me. I'd been four years old at the time.

I took an unsteady breath. First, a reminder of how much I hated heights. Now, a reminder of how much I hated travel over dangerous, rocky terrain. This was shaping up to be a lovely night so far.

"Are you all right, Frella?" Nyx asked in his barely-there voice. "You're shaking."

I dragged myself back to the here and now. "Yeah, no. I'm fine," I lied. "Just a bit chilly. Are we ready to press on yet?"

Eldris' eyes wandered down from my face to a place not too far above the water line. Where, I realized, certain parts of me were, in fact, proclaiming that they were a bit chilly. Proclaiming it rather clearly through my soaking wet, white linen tunic.

"At least they float, okay?" I snapped.

Dark eyes jerked back to my face, a bit sheepishly if I was any judge. But, on the positive side, the flush climbing up my chest and neck warmed me up.

"Perhaps we should get moving," Aristede suggested.

"Perhaps we should," I muttered, and started slogging upstream.

Eldris' earlier assessment was fairly accurate. There were stretches where the sand and rocks had accumulated and we could walk rather than wade. There were stretches where we had to feel our way along the river bottom and try not to slip on the steep drop-away. And there was the big, invisible hole where I, with my stubborn insistence in stalking off to take the lead, promptly disappeared underwater, barely managing to keep the saddlebags from taking a dunking with me as I held them outstretched with one arm over my head.

"Thought those tits were supposed to float," Eldris called from behind me, once I'd surfaced, sputtering and coughing up a good lungful of river water. If I hadn't needed my free arm to keep from going under again and drowning, I'd have tested whether rude hand gestures were ubiquitous across cultural lines.

Eventually, we made it to a place where the canyon opened out, a steep trail leading up to the higher elevations. We stopped long enough to rest for a few minutes and put our boots back on. Despite my years of going barefoot around the village half the time, I suspected that the soles of my feet would be planning their revenge on me for the next week, at least.

"What about all the ravines and crevasses up there?" I asked warily, eyeing the uplands at the top of the trail.

"Mostly behind us now," Aristede said.

Mostly. Oh, good.

I wrung out my tunic as best I could, only to have Aristede's mare soak me again with a violent, full body shake. Eldris snorted, but was smart enough not to laugh outright.

"Hop up in the saddle," he said. "You take the mare, and Nyx, you can have my gelding. Ari and I'll hang on behind for the climb."

It made sense—Nyx and I were the lightest, and it was easier for a horse to pull a heavy load up an incline than carry it. As long as they were trained to accept it without getting pissy and kicking at you, holding onto a horse's tail was a good way to get up a steep hill.

We stowed the supplies and headed up, reaching the top a few minutes later. From there, our travel did become considerably less fraught, despite my paranoid scanning of the footing ahead of us in the uncertain light of the moon. To spare the horses as much as possible, we switched off riding and walking instead of trying to ride double again.

For the most part, the climb was steady but not as ridiculously steep as the trail up from the river had been. It was still wearing, though, to someone more used to riding than walking. Now that we were beyond the reach of all but the most stubborn and prescient pursuers, we did stop every few hours to eat and grab a bit of restless sleep.

Still, it was a grueling journey, made more so as the air grew thinner in the higher elevation. I'd experienced that effect before when crossing the Southern Mountains on Eburos to travel between Draebard and my brother's home in Rhyth, so I wasn't surprised when my head began to ache and my breathing labored, even with steady walking.

The landscape changed, growing greener, with trees and shrubs burgeoning amongst the plentiful springs and mountain streams. It was beautiful, even if I was too tired to appreciate it to the fullest extent.

We walked and rode through the day and into the next night, taking a final rest for a couple of hours beneath a stone overhang. We'd chanced a fire, the others being confident now that we were well beyond the threat of Prince Oblisii and his guards. I awoke abruptly, certain that I'd heard the rustle of large wings overhead.

"What was that?" I slurred.

I was exhausted and still half asleep, but I could have sworn I saw Eldris exchange a look with Aristede before the latter shrugged and said,

"Who knows? There are all manner of things up here. Whatever it was, it's gone now."

It might have been gone, but the horses pawed restlessly and were skittish for the next stretch of travel. The landscape changed again, forest interspersed with grassy valleys where our mounts stretched their heads down and ripped at any tufts they could reach as they walked along.

I judged it was getting close to dawn when we crossed one such valley with a still, spring-fed lake mirroring the stars above. A rocky cliff bounded the far side of the grassy expanse, and I could see a strange orange glow emanating from it. I blinked, trying to force the view to make sense in my sleepy mind. It took an embarrassingly long time to realize that it was firelight coming from inside the mouth of a cave.

"There he is," Eldris said. "Told you we could make it here in a bit more than a day."

"So you did," Aristede agreed easily. "Now, do we think he's awake in there?"

"No telling." Eldris whistled, a louder version of the call Aristede had used at the window of the room in the Purple Cloak. A horse nickered from somewhere out of sight in the dark—presumably Rayth's stallion hobbled nearby to graze at night.

We continued to approach, Eldris and Aristede whistling the same complicated, birdlike warble at intervals. Eventually, a similar whistle sounded from the cave. Nyx and I had been riding, and we dismounted as a figure appeared at the entrance to the cave. He was silhouetted by firelight, his shirt half-untucked and a crossbow held casually in one hand, hanging at his side.

"What the bloody blazes are you two doing up here?" Rayth asked, sounding either sleep-befuddled or hung-over. Or both, I thought uncharitably. His posture tensed as he noticed that there were four people at his doorstep, not two.

"We found a bit of trouble in Safaad," Eldris said. "Decided to bring it along with us. More fun that way."

Rayth stood unmoving for another beat before he turned and retreated into the cave, which appeared to be massive. "Get inside," he threw over his shoulder. "And then you can explain this properly."

"I believe that was to be your job," Aristede murmured to Eldris as he brushed past. "As we agreed at the inn."

I followed the two of them, aware that Nyx was hanging back nervously. The inside of the cave had obviously been in use for some time. There was nothing fancy—no surprise since anything brought here would presumably have to be lugged along the same tortuous route the four of us had just ascended. Still, there were supplies and basic furnishings made from local materials.

There was also a rather startling amount of game hanging against the back wall—fowl, rabbits, what looked like beavers or muskrats, and even a decently sized stag. Apparently, we would at least be eating well while we were here.

Rayth's eyes landed on me as I entered the cave. "Oh," he said flatly. "So it's *that* kind of trouble."

"Nice to see you, too," I replied, my mood not terribly buoyant after the last few days.

Rayth grunted and scrubbed his free hand through his tousled black hair. I heard footsteps behind me as Nyx finally decided to brave the circle of firelight and join us. What happened next registered more as a confused jumble of movement and sound, rather than a sequence of discrete events.

Both Nyx and Rayth froze as though turned to stone, staring at each other as if they'd each seen a ghost. The blood drained from Nyx's face, even as Rayth's grew ruddy, rage twisting his handsome features.

"*You*—" Nyx gasped, as though the word had been punched from him.

Rayth said nothing, but murder flashed behind his eyes. The crossbow that had been hanging casually by his right thigh swung up to point at Nyx's heart, and my mind registered the bolt nocked in place and ready to fly.

Without even thinking, I stepped into the path of the arrow and glared into that coldly murderous gaze. A throwing knife was already in my hand. Quick as a flash, my wrist snapped and the point of the small dagger was embedded in the meat of Rayth's left bicep.

He yelped in surprise, his other hand jerking uncontrollably as I had known it would. With a twang, the crossbow bolt shot harmlessly over my head, the metal point clattering against the rock wall above the cave entrance. Behind me, I heard Nyx hare away into the gray pre-dawn, boots pounding against the hard-packed earth.

"Don't point weapons at people who saved my life," I growled at Rayth. He was gaping at me, open-mouthed, his right hand clamped to his injured arm and the crossbow lying at his feet where it had fallen. I pinned first Eldris, and then Aristede with my angry gaze. "Keep him from following us, or I'll aim someplace more vital next time."

They, too, had apparently been rendered speechless. I pivoted on my heel before they could recover, and stormed off after Nyx.

THIRTEEN

Nyx was a darker smudge against the gray of early morning as he ran through the valley. In his panic, he was retracing the same path we'd followed to the cave, the grass bent and broken from our horses' recent passage.

I jogged after him, cursing my exhaustion and sore feet; hoping that he would be similarly unable to keep up such a pace for long. Indeed, as he reached the wooded area opposite the cliff wall and cave, his gait slowed to an agitated walk and I began to catch up to him.

The light was growing brighter as I followed him into the trees. I'd been trusting our route to Eldris and Aristede in the dark as we ascended, but now I could see that our path had followed an animal trail. Nyx's overwrought state apparently precluded his being quiet, and I could easily hear him crashing through the branches and underbrush ahead.

I chewed on my lower lip, briefly debating the merits of marking our trail versus the merits of making it more difficult for Rayth to follow us. Of course, Rayth had other things to worry about right now, and while this was a path, of sorts, it was intersected by numerous other animal trails. The very last thing we needed was to get lost out here.

I still had four blades left. Pulling one of them from my belt, I used the edge to gouge an arrow into the bark of a twisted tree trunk, pointing back the way I'd come. I picked out a tree further along the trail but within my line of sight and did the same thing, repeating the action over and over while trying not to let it slow me down too much.

Ahead of me, the sounds of cracking twigs and scuffling steps halted abruptly. As I grew nearer, though, I could make out the sound of ragged breathing — that gut-twisting sound someone makes when they would probably be sobbing if they could get enough air into their lungs to do so.

The trail opened out into a small clearing. The sun wasn't nearly high enough yet to penetrate the mountainous terrain directly, but it was light enough now to see detail in my surroundings. Nyx had made it about a dozen steps into the glade and collapsed to his knees, his spine bowed under some invisible weight. He clutched handfuls of the tufted grass beneath him, the slender blades twisting and tearing in his grip.

An ache rose in my throat, for all that I had no idea what was going on. Seeing him like this pricked the sense of protectiveness that Nyx seemed to engender in me. Even before this latest mystery, he came across as so... *broken*. And yet so beautiful, as well. I wanted to fix him. To glue his shattered pieces together and make him whole.

Dangerous, my inner voice counseled.

I thought of Aristede with his silver tongue and cold, steely eyes... of Rayth, his body pinning mine to the ground as his hard cock pressed against my hip. I was surrounding myself with dangerous men. Eldris was the only straightforward one of the lot. Part of me wished he was here—Nyx had seemed oddly unafraid of him. But part of me knew that of all of us, I was best equipped to deal with… whatever this was.

"I'm alone, Nyx," I said, still poised at the edge of the woods. "I told the others to keep Rayth back at the cave."

Cautiously, I crossed to where Nyx still knelt hunched on the ground, unmoving except for his heaving chest. When he didn't bolt at my approach, I sank to sit cross-legged in front of him, leaving a bit of space between us. My sore muscles protested the movement, but I ignored them—waiting silently to see what Nyx would do next.

He didn't change position. Didn't meet my eyes. Above us, the sky shifted from turquoise to cerulean, the color more brilliant than I could ever remember seeing. I had no idea how long we sat there until some of the tension started to drain from Nyx's posture and he shifted onto his rump, drawing his knees up to his chin and hiding behind the barrier they formed.

"His name's not Rayth," he whispered eventually.

I remained silent, waiting, and was rewarded when he peeked up at me to gauge my reaction. It was the first time I'd gotten a clear, close-up view of his extraordinary eyes in daylight. They were brown, yes, but with tiny streaks the color of molten copper running through them. The most striking thing, though, was that irregular ring of mossy green surrounding his irises. I'd never seen eyes like them.

I would have been quite content to stare into them, trying to memorize the pattern of color, but his dark lashes swept down, shielding them as his gaze dropped once more.

"How do you know each other?" I asked quietly. The answering silence was long enough that I began to wonder if he would reply at all.

"I… was his steward." Nyx's voice was hoarse, as though he'd been screaming. "I was sixteen. He was in the cavalry, and I was training to be, someday." He paused, swallowing with an audible click of the throat. "There… was a battle and… I… ran away."

I digested that. Continental armies were quite different than the loosely organized warrior class of the northern Eburosi tribes I'd grown up in, I knew. But even back home in Draebard, an apprentice warrior who fled the battleground would bring shame on himself and his family.

Rayth's face hadn't shown contempt, though. Every line of his expression had conveyed the intent to kill without thought. There was more to the story, and I waited to see if it would emerge.

"The fight… was… going badly. He and his comrades were nearly surrounded, and several of them had already been unhorsed. He screamed for fresh weapons…" Nyx's gaze drifted up, but it was far away, seeing something from the past, rather than me and the glade around us.

That muffled sound of large wings catching the air came from somewhere above—the same noise I'd heard earlier in the dark. I jerked my head up, scanning the skies curiously, but there was nothing in my field of vision.

Nyx appeared not to have noticed. "I grabbed whatever steel I could carry and started forward, but… everything went gray and fuzzy at the edges. I couldn't breathe. I wasn't on the battlefield anymore. I was—" He cut himself off and shook his head, trying to clear it.

"I don't know what happened after that," he continued, the words flowing faster now. "The next thing I remember, I was hiding under a fallen tree in the woods, and the battle was over. We'd been leagues away from Safaad, near the borderlands. I ran away, and didn't stop running until I was in the mountains. I lived there for more than a year. Closer to two, I guess. It wasn't this area, but it wasn't all that different, really. I only came down to the nearest villages when I needed to steal something I couldn't get otherwise."

I was silent, running his words through my head. If Nyx had abandoned Rayth and his comrades without the weapons they needed when they were overmatched in battle, it was likely that people had died as a result. And with someone like Rayth—bitter and wine-soaked, pent up behind that dry, acerbic exterior—I could easily imagine that resulting in the scene we'd just fled.

"I can't go back to that cave," Nyx said. "I'm sorry I ever agreed to come here."

My hands itched to reach out to him. Maybe I should have felt contempt for Nyx after his confession of boyhood cowardice, but the damaged man in front of me looked like someone who had already suffered at great length for his shortcomings. Besides, even now, something inside me whispered that there was more to his tale than a single moment of faintheartedness during battle.

"I'm sorry I dragged you here," I told him, trying to keep any trace of judgment from my tone. "But I don't want you to go."

His eyes flew to mine as though I'd surprised him. He drew breath to say something, but the noise from above came again. "What was that?" he asked instead, scrambling to his feet.

I followed suit, scanning the skies. My eyes skittered over a gray shape, unable to make sense of it at first. It was… too large. A hand grasped my upper arm convulsively, dragging me back a few steps as the great, winged creature circling the clearing spiraled downward. The air buffeted around us as it flapped to slow its descent. Hind legs hit the ground with a solid thump, followed by forelegs, and a scaled head craned forward to regard us from atop a graceful, swanlike neck.

My breath caught in my lungs, Nyx's fingers gouging bruises into my upper arm as he tried to drag me backwards into the woods. I shook him off, staring at the animal before us.

"Oh, my gods," I whispered, staring into gimlet eyes the color of aquamarine.

Nyx was breathing with ragged gasps behind me.

"I… I can't…" he croaked. He tried to grab me again, but I tore his hand away, moving out of reach. "Frella… for the love of all that's holy, *run!*"

I didn't run, though the sound of retreating footsteps disappearing into the woods told me that he had. I didn't want to run. Running would mean taking my eyes off the impossible creature before me.

It was roughly the size of a small horse, but far longer from nose to tail. It had large, membranous wings, four legs, and a graceful head like a cross between a stag and a snake. Scales covered most of its body aside from the wing membranes. They were mostly of a dull, nondescript grayish color, except for parts of its head and the back of its neck, where they were a shiny, pearlescent white. The white areas looked newer, less worn, like maybe the scales were in the process of shedding and being replaced, like a bird's feathers.

But the *eyes*. They were large. Almond-shaped. A shade of shimmering, depthless blue-green that put the finest cut gemstones to shame. And they were looking straight at me. Straight... *into* me.

The impossible dragon tilted its elegant head, regarding me curiously. My body had petrified into immobility. I did not move a muscle as it walked toward me, step by step. Its gait was something between a reptilian glide and a great, hunting cat.

Was I being hunted? Was I mad not to have followed Nyx's example and run for my life? I might well be one well-aimed gout of flame away from a messy, agonizing death. But if that were the case, would running now make any difference?

The smell of sulfur and wood smoke wafted to my nostrils as the dragon scented the air around me, its breath like the sound of bellows. I stared into those bottomless blue-green eyes, feeling that if I could just see deep enough, I would find the answers to all my questions.

The dragon snuffled around my head and shoulders, warm air currents tickling my skin. Curiously, it nudged at the tangled mass of hair hanging down my back, nosing into it.

The gemstones, I realized.

Before I could pause to wonder if it wanted them or was just curious about them, the dragon snorted and jerked away. Warm smoke swirled around me, and I coughed, waving a hand in an attempt to clear the air. The dragon had stiffened, staring fixedly at the trailhead Nyx and I had emerged from earlier.

"Frella!" called a familiar voice, though not one I was used to hearing shouting at me.

Aristede ran into the clearing and skidded to a halt, staring in shock at the scene. The dragon leapt back from me and gave an earsplitting shriek before taking to the air with a powerful beat of its wings. I stared, slack-jawed, as it disappeared into the sky and vanished beyond the tree line, another swirl of wind rustling the grass around us in its wake.

"That was a dragon," I said with unnatural calmness.

"I don't believe this," Aristede said faintly.

I turned to him, assuming that he was sharing my shock over the existence of dragons when they were all supposed to be dead. Whatever I might have said was interrupted by Eldris' arrival. He was out of breath.

"Was that—?" he asked.

"It was," Aristede said, confusing me. "The white male. It came right up to her."

"Huh?" I asked, blinking as I tried to retrieve my wits.

"Did you catch Nyx?" Aristede continued, still addressing Eldris, who shook his head.

"Nah, he got away. He was running like all of the ancestor-demons from the shadow realm were on his heels."

"What are you both talking about?" I asked in bewilderment.

"Once we got Rayth calmed down and his arm bandaged, we followed your markings on the trail," Eldris said. "We were almost to the clearing when we heard wings overhead."

"A few moments later, Nyx came barreling down the path, full-tilt," Aristede continued dryly. "When he saw us, he charged into the underbrush and headed down a side trail. Eldris took off after him while I came to find you and make sure you were all right."

"You knew about the dragon," I accused, still sounding way calmer than I really felt.

They shared a glance. It was the same kind of glance I'd seen them share when Eldris first suggested bringing me into the mountains, and when we'd heard the wings overhead in the dark.

"I still have four throwing knives, you realize," I pointed out, by way of motivation for them to stop looking at each other meaningfully, and start making mouth sounds.

"The male has shown no interest in approaching humans up until now," Aristede said gently. "In fact, he's been positively aggressive at times."

"That's interesting, I suppose," I said, "but it's not an answer to my question. *You know about the dragons.*"

"That was a statement, not a question," Aristede pointed out.

I ground my teeth.

"Ari, mate, I'm not patching you up if she decides to put a knife someplace unfortunate," Eldris said with a sigh. "We've known about the dragons for the last two years, Frella. We've been trying to tame them. Three of the females are starting to come around, but there's another female we can't even get near, and the male wants nothing to do with us."

"That's…" I began, unsure how the sentence should end. *Amazing? Unlikely? Surreal?* "…insane."

"Come back to the cave with us," Aristede said. "We'll talk more."

"Yeah," I agreed. "Let's go back to the cave."

We started to trudge along the trail, marked with my hastily scratched arrows. We'd gotten about halfway along its length when I suddenly stopped, a relevant fact finally percolating into my fuzzy, wool-wrapped thoughts.

Nyx was gone.

He'd said he was leaving, and the dragon came before I had a chance to try talking him out of it. Or even deciding if it was a good idea to try and talk him out of it. A familiar heaviness settled over my heart.

Of course Nyx had left. Everyone left sooner or later. He had just chosen to do it sooner. It was best that way, right? Why should I even care that a coward who had run away and gotten people killed was gone? Running away was apparently what he *did*. At least no one had died this time.

The tough words, silent though they were, did nothing to lift the sudden weight on my chest. I didn't want to accept that I would never get to study those green-ringed eyes again, or try to uncover the untold story behind his too-quiet voice and the way he flinched from unexpected contact.

Eldris paused and looked over his shoulder. "What's wrong, Trouble?"

I swallowed against the tightness of my throat. "Nothing's wrong," I said. "I'm right behind you."

FOURTEEN

"**Y**ou haven't asked how badly you skewered Rayth with that throwing knife," Aristede observed as we started across the windswept valley.

I scowled, my mood not having improved as I trekked back on sore feet toward a man I was royally pissed at right now. "Not as badly as he intended to skewer Nyx with his crossbow bolt, or I assume you two wouldn't be here playing nice with me."

Eldris snorted. "You don't realize it yet, Frella, but you may have just become the most valuable person in Utrea," he said, and I scowled harder. "Rayth'll manage, though. The blade didn't bite into the muscle too badly. Mostly, it slid under the skin. Ari wrapped it and put it in a sling. We left him with the last wineskin, and I expect the combination of those two things will have kept him from wandering off in our absence."

"I should've aimed lower," I muttered. Heaving in a cleansing breath, I raised my voice back to its normal level. "What did he tell you about Nyx? I assume you asked while you were patching him up."

Aristede sighed, and shot me a sidelong glance. "That his real name is Leannyck, and he was Rayth's steward in the cavalry several years ago. He lost his nerve in a battle during the Southern Uprising and ran off, leaving Rayth and his squad weaponless while surrounded by the enemy. Three of Rayth's comrades died in the fight."

The twisted up knot in my chest and stomach grew more tangled, but I kept quiet. The two men's stories agreed, and the desire for revenge was a powerful motivator for violence.

We were approaching the cave now. I was surprised to see Rayth out front, awkwardly strapping supplies onto his horse, which stood saddled and ready.

"Rayth, what are you doing?" Eldris asked, sounding tired.

"What does it look like I'm doing?" Rayth replied.

"Your arm—" Eldris began.

"Fuck my arm. You obviously didn't catch him, so I'm going after him. Was he with her?" Rayth's acid-filled gaze swept over me.

"Now, just a damned minute!" I snapped, stepping forward only to be caught and held by the upper arm.

Eldris tugged me back against his body. His voice whispered against the shell of my ear, so soft no one else could hear it. "Trust us, sweet thing."

I clamped my lips shut tightly, not sure if I could trust them in this or not.

"He was," Aristede was saying, "but he ran off. They were headed down the easternmost trailhead on the far side of the valley, and when he saw us, he darted onto one of the paths on the north side. The ones that head back down toward the lowlands."

My brow furrowed. That didn't sound right. The path we'd taken had been more toward the western edge of the valley, and I was quite certain that all of the side trails near where we'd found the dragon had been leading uphill, not down. Eldris gave my arm a warning squeeze, and I understood in a flash that Aristede was sending Rayth on a goose chase.

I jerked my arm free of Eldris and stalked up to Rayth, ready to play my part. "Why don't you just leave Nyx alone?" I poked him sharply in the chest, and he stared down at my finger as though surprised that I would dare do such a thing. "He's got an hour's head start on you anyway. You'll never catch him."

"There's another small point you should be aware of before you leave," Aristede said smoothly.

Rayth glanced at him in obvious irritation. "And that is?"

"We found the white dragon cozied up to our girl, here. He was snufflin' away at her hair when Aristede charged into the clearing—friendly as you please," Eldris said.

Rayth's eyes flew back to me, surprise warring with something that almost looked like... outrage? I glared back.

"You know we wouldn't joke about something so serious, my friend," Aristede said soothingly. "And you're well aware of what it means. We really need to sit down and talk."

Rayth's jaw worked. "You two sit down and talk to her, damn it. I'm going after the deserter. I've no desire to share a cave with this knife-wielding hellion at the moment, and I'm sure the feeling is mutual."

"It most definitely is," I grated out. "Have fun playing hide-and-go-seek in the mountains."

Rayth turned his back on me without a word, gathering up his reins in his good hand and swinging into the saddle. It was a reasonably impressive feat with one arm in a sling. Once settled, he looked down at me.

"What did the worthless deserter tell you?" Rayth asked, surprising me.

"That he was your steward, and he fled a battle, leaving you and your comrades surrounded by the enemy," I told him.

He cocked a sharp black brow. "At least he was honest."

"And that your name isn't Rayth," I finished, fishing for a reaction.

He regarded me steadily for a long moment.

"On the contrary," he said eventually. "Rayth is the only name remaining to me."

With that, he reined his stallion around and jabbed his heels into its sides, leaving me standing in the dust as he galloped away.

"That certainly went well," Aristede said with fake cheer.

I blinked weary eyes at him, my exhaustion catching up with me all at once. "You sent him looking in the wrong direction. Thank you."

"Told you to trust us," Eldris rumbled.

Aristede flashed me half a smile, but the expression was worn. "It seemed the best way to keep a nice enough lad from being murdered, while also giving Rayth a chance to work off some of his pique. I don't expect we'll see him again until tomorrow."

"Probably not," Eldris agreed. "He's a stubborn bastard."

I looked between them. "You're not worried about him being out there at night with his arm in a sling?"

Aristede huffed a breath of laughter. "Hardly. He was a soldier for more than a decade, Frella. I've seen him hold off enemy forces for days while camped in hostile territory with a broken foot, protecting comrades who were too badly injured to rise."

I digested that, aware that in order to have seen it, Aristede must have been one of those injured comrades. I'd known, on some level, that there must be reasons these two maintained a friendship with such a bitter, prickly asshole—but this was the first real glance I'd had into those reasons.

"He'll be fine," Eldris agreed. "Honestly, I'm more worried about the lad. Maybe he did act the coward when he was a kid, but I kind of liked him."

"Me, too," I murmured. "I expect he'll be all right, though. I gave him one of my knives, and he lived up here alone for a long time, apparently. It's not cold or raining. He knows how to survive."

It was as good of an outcome as I could have hoped for, under the circumstances. The pair was headed in opposite directions, and both of them could handle themselves. I tried to tell myself that Rayth could fall down a hole for all I cared, but thinking things like that brought to mind too many other people in my life who had ridden away and not come back.

"Come on," Aristede said kindly. "We're all exhausted and hungry. Eldris took care of the horses and hobbled them near the lake while I was bandaging Rayth's arm, so there's nothing much that needs doing right now. Looks like it will just be us for the next little while."

The knots inside me finally began to unwind. I was comfortable with these two. I trusted them. And for now, it looked like there would be no new crises rearing their ugly heads for a bit. We were well away from prince Oblisii's reach, and the valley was safe and peaceful.

Also, there were fucking *dragons*. Oh. My. Gods.

I let the others lead the way into the cave. Eldris rummaged for some food and drink, passing it out to us before flopping down on one of the bedrolls with a groan. "I could sleep for a week," he said.

So could I, but I needed more answers first. "Talk and eat first. Then sleep. I think at this point I deserve a more detailed explanation of what the blazes is going on."

"That you do," Aristede agreed. "And also an apology for my reluctance to bring you here. If I'd known…" He trailed off, shaking his head.

"This is why you should always listen to my ideas," Eldris teased, and Aristede graced him with a rueful smile.

"Apparently so. At any rate, the short version of a long story is this. A little more than two years ago, Rayth decided he'd had enough of soldiering and left the army all three of us had been serving in."

"The king's army?" I asked, around a mouthful of smoked fowl.

"No," Aristede said.

I tilted my head. "You were mercenaries?"

Eldris barked a laugh. "Still are, sweet thing. Swords for hire, that's us."

Aristede settled back and continued. "Rayth left, and traveled up here to… get some time to himself, I suppose you'd say."

I nodded, finding it interesting that both Rayth and Nyx had fled to the mountains, albeit at different points in time and for different reasons.

"It wasn't in this cave, but another one not far from here. Rayth stumbled on a cache of dragon eggs that had somehow escaped the bounty hunters. Most of them were cracked or shattered, but about a dozen seemed undamaged. It was reckless of him, but he set fire to the forest around the cave and fled downwind until the flames burned themselves out."

I shivered, thinking of the stories my brother Favian had told me about the Battle at the Western

Pass, where Eburosi forces had lured an invading Alyrion army onto a mountainside and then set fire to it. Still, I was rapt as Aristede continued the tale.

"When he came back, it was to find that five of the eggs had hatched successfully. The others weren't viable. He fed the hatchlings on rabbit meat and whatever else he could hunt or trap. But dragonettes — young dragons — grow quickly."

"And they're unruly beasts, as well," Eldris put in wryly.

"Very," Aristede agreed. "As soon as they started flying, they left the cave and began to disappear for longer and longer intervals. Rayth knew very well the importance of what he had. He also knew the danger inherent in it. He realized he couldn't deal with the situation on his own. So he ventured into the city long enough to hire a messenger to track us down in the borderlands."

"Imagine our surprise," Eldris put in, "when we received a mysterious message from the wine-soaked son of a bitch who'd left us with barely a by-your-leave, begging us to come meet him in this little no-name village at the base of the mountains. We probably would've laughed it off, but the crazy bastard had managed to pique our curiosity."

Aristede shrugged agreement. "We were both tiring of battle-for-hire. Perhaps we were looking for an excuse. Whatever the case, we never expected the reason for the summons to be that our old comrade had stumbled on the last five dragons in existence."

I could just imagine. "So you came and found Rayth with his dragons. And that was, what? A couple of years ago?"

"About that," Eldris said.

"What happened since then?" I asked.

"Since then," Aristede replied, "We've been splitting our time between earning enough coin to keep ourselves supplied, and coming up here to try and tame the recalcitrant beasts. With mixed success."

"Gladya talked a bit about dragons when you were camped with us that night," Eldris said. "She told you about how they're just wild beasts until they bond with a human, right?"

"Yes," I said, remembering the conversation.

"Well, there's five dragons, you see? A male and four females," Eldris went on. "Only, they're starting to get big now, and range farther afield. They'll get bigger yet. Much bigger. And eventually, some poor sod wandering around in the mountains to hunt or harvest lumber is going to see a great, flying beast breathing fire into the sky. At which point, we'll all be in the shit."

"Succinctly put," Aristede said.

I nodded slowly. "So you three are trying to bond with them, and then they'll be able to understand the necessity of hiding themselves away from other humans."

"More or less," said Eldris. "But there's only three of us, and we can only bond with one dragon each. Not that we've been able to do even that much yet, mind you."

"They've already developed preferences, though," Aristede elaborated. "We each have a female that will approach us, and tolerate our touch. Sometimes they even seem friendly, but it's still a far cry from a soul-bond."

I shivered a bit, feeling a wash of superstitious fear at the idea of melding with another creature so thoroughly that their death would cause your death. What would it be like? How could you wake each day knowing that it might be the day you lost part of your soul?

"There's a fourth female," Eldris said. "A little green one who's shy as anything. But we haven't caught so much as a glimpse of her in quite some time. She might be dead."

Aristede's eyes landed on me. "And then, there's the male. The one who wouldn't look twice at a human."

"Until now," Eldris finished.

FIFTEEN

Connections were clicking together in my mind. One male dragon. A single chance for more eggs… more dragons… no matter how many females there were. And the male had approached me, after scorning Rayth, Aristede, and Eldris. My thoughts went blank, my mind calling an abrupt halt to the day's proceedings.

"I need to sleep," I said without preamble. "I can't take in anything else right now."

"That's fair," Eldris said, stifling a yawn. "It's been quite a couple of days."

"Do we need a watch?" I asked, dreading the answer.

Aristede shook his head. "No, there's no need to worry about it. It's daylight, and I'll build up the campfire to discourage any… non-fire-breathing animals from wandering in. Besides, I'll wake up if there's any disturbance. Or possibly even if there's not."

The surreality of the situation struck me anew, but I shook it off. "Good." I eyed Rayth's bedroll and my lips curled downward. No way was I interested in Rayth walking in unexpectedly to discover me curled up in his blanket. "Can I share a bedroll with one of you?"

Aristede waved a lazy hand—shooing me in Eldris' direction, though there was a twinkle in his eye. "Bed down with him. He sleeps like a log, whereas I'm likely to kick you accidentally. Besides, he's very cuddly."

"Ass," Eldris groused.

I was past arguing, and it wasn't like Eldris was *protesting*, as such. I finished my food and took a swig of clean mountain spring water from the waterskin. Figuring it was finally safe to do so, I tugged off my boots. After plaiting my hair in a messy braid so it wouldn't get everywhere while I slept, I nudged Eldris with a toe.

"Budge up," I ordered.

He scooted back, making a space for me. It wasn't hot like it had been in the Utrean desert, but it was still pleasantly warm. Since it was still early morning, I assumed it would only get warmer. So I forewent the blanket, using it as an added layer of padding on the hard-packed dirt floor, rather than a cover.

"Wake me if anything interesting happens," I muttered as Eldris settled on his side at my back.

"Sleep well, Frella," Aristede said quietly.

And I did.

✦

I awoke much later, with the fuzzy feeling that comes from hours of deep sleep. My resting place had somehow become a lot more comfortable while I'd slept. It was also... well... *breathing*.

I pried sticky eyelids open to discover that Eldris had rolled onto his back at some point, and I had rolled over so that my head was propped in the crook of his muscular shoulder, one of my arms and one of my legs thrown over his body possessively. His arm wrapped around my back, his large hand a warm weight on the dip of my waist.

"This is nice," he said, the waking roughness of his voice rumbling against my cheek.

It certainly was. As many nagging worries as were hovering around me, waiting for an excuse to dive back in, I thought I could get used to waking in such a manner.

"Very nice, indeed," came Aristede's voice from somewhere behind me. "I'm quite overcome with jealousy."

The words were light, his tone definitely sounding more appreciative than jealous. Something inside me tightened pleasantly at the idea of Aristede watching us sleep, our bodies twined together. What would happen, I wondered, if I rolled on top of Eldris right now? Would he let me kiss him? Was he hard for me? Would he rock his hips against mine?

Would Aristede enjoy watching that as much as he'd enjoyed watching us sleep? Would he… join us?

Godsdamnit, why did these two have to be so bloody appealing?

Eldris shifted beneath me. "What's that racket?" he asked, scrubbing his free hand over his face.

I'd missed the rustling noises coming from outside until he said something, but now that I was focusing, I could hear them clearly. I straightened from my sprawl against Eldris, the pleasant lassitude and warmth from my drowsy fantasies dissipating like mist.

"The girls are here," Aristede said. He caught my eye. "Ready to meet some more dragons, Frella?"

I blinked. "Oh—I am *so* ready," I told him, excitement driving the last wisps of sleep from my body.

Eldris grinned up at me, and I had to fight the urge to kiss him. He rolled upright, muscles rippling. "Then dragons you shall meet. Though you might wanna stay back at first. Not sure how they'll take to a stranger in the weyr."

"Weyr?" I echoed.

"Den," Aristede explained. "Specifically, this cave. Now… it looks like Rayth has been busy in our absence, at least."

He was inspecting the back wall, from which he pulled down a couple of large fowl and a brace of hares. I realized that Rayth had been hunting game to feed the dragons, not us, and felt stupid. Of course, feeding the beasts was a logical way to keep them friendly and tame.

I caught my breath as a pointed snout poked into the cave entrance, joined shortly by a second and a third. Long necks jostled and twined together as the three dragons scented the air. Like the male, they were mostly gray, but had irregular patches of varying sizes on their heads and necks displaying much brighter scales. I saw scarlet, some mix of blue and indigo, and jet black.

"Hello, girls," Eldris said, his rumbly voice low and pleasant.

The blue dragon let out a little chirping noise and crept forward a step, but the black one hissed and pulled away from the entrance in a mad scramble of flapping wings. The noise of flapping grew more distant as it flew away.

"Did I scare her?" I asked, contrite.

"She's Rayth's," Aristede said.

"Ah," I replied. "So you're saying she's pissy and prone to bouts of overreaction."

Eldris chuckled. "No, she's just not interested if he isn't here. They're rather particular."

And squirrely, I thought, but didn't say—remembering how fast the male had taken off when Aristede arrived and startled him. It was hard to reconcile the vision of devastating war beasts with these skittish youngsters, but perhaps that's what the others had meant about the soul bonds. Without them, dragons were wild animals like any other—concerned only with survival.

"C'mon, pets," Eldris coaxed. "Come and say hello, and then you can have your breakfast."

The blue female shook herself like a dog and flapped her massive wings once before carefully furling them against her body. Then she slipped into the cave, all serpentine grace. The red dragon followed, using her sister's body as a shield between herself and me, not letting me get a good look from my spot at the side of the cave.

"Shyness does not become you, beautiful," Aristede chided, his normally velvet voice growing even smoother and deeper, doing strange things to my insides.

The red dragon ducked her head under her sister's arched neck, fixing me with a ruby eye for a long moment before finally detaching herself from her companion. With a soft rumbling noise that somehow conveyed pleasure, she pushed toward Aristede, nudging him with her scaly nose. He smiled and scratched the small crest at the back of her skull.

I watched, enchanted, as the pair of men greeted the dragons with low words and caresses. *Lucky girls*, I thought, a smile tugging at my lips. I stayed put, sensing that any move I made toward the beasts would send them flapping away in a huff. I'd spent enough time in Draebard watching Carivel tame skittish horses to know that you couldn't force an animal's trust—you had to earn it.

Sometimes, the best way to earn that trust was to respect their space, and respect their fear of you. Especially when they might breathe fire at you if they felt cornered.

That point was brought home when Aristede's dragon started sniffing at the fowl he was holding. He took one of the carcasses and tossed it toward the cave entrance. Before I could blink, a gout of flame shot out, roasting the bird before it hit the ground. The red female leapt forward in a playful pounce and started tearing into the meat, while the indigo one peered around Eldris' body and gave an odd little bleat.

"Go on, then," Eldris said with a nudge.

Aristede tossed the other fowl into the air, and the dragon repeated her sister's trick of midair cookery before starting in on her meal. The two men repeated the performance with the hares, and before long, not a bone or a feather remained in evidence of the small feast.

When the meat was gone, the dragons started fussing with each other—play fighting, I thought. Without a backward glance at their human benefactors, they shoved and wrestled their way out of the cave. A few moments later, I heard the flapping of great wings. I walked up to join Eldris and Aristede outside the entrance, watching as the large shapes grew smaller and smaller before disappearing.

"You have dragons," I said quietly. When that didn't elicit the kind of response that I felt would be appropriate, I turned to them, pointing between them and emphasizing my words more forcefully. "Aristede. Eldris. *You*… have *dragons*."

Eldris' eyes crinkled at the corner, but his expression was a bit wistful. "We don't have them yet, sweet thing. You saw. I think they mostly just see us as kitchen slaves."

"It's disheartening that after two years, we haven't forged more of a connection," Aristede explained. "No doubt it doesn't help that we sometimes have to leave for days or even weeks at a time to refill our coffers."

I nodded. Nyx might have survived up here on his own, with occasional pilferage from villages in the foothills. But horses still had to be shod, tack repaired, clothing and boots mended or replaced. And while there was safe water here to drink, it must be hard to hunt enough game for three grown men and three hungry dragons. I also knew that, depending on the season, finding enough plant-based food in wild areas like this could be harder than it looked. Lean meat only went so far.

"I think what you've done here is amazing," I said. "Maybe it's just a matter of patience. They're obviously fond of you—and even loyal, based on the reaction of the black dragon when she realized Rayth wasn't in the cave."

"I hope you're right," Eldris said. "They won't be small forever, and eventually someone's going to notice them."

Small? Good gods, they were already as tall at the shoulder as I was. I let it go, though.

"I'm sure it will work out," I said with finality.

No way would I let myself think about these beautiful, amazing creatures being hunted. Instead, I tried to turn my attention to more practical matters now that the afternoon's excitement seemed to be over. "It's later than I thought. Is the lake safe to bathe in?"

"Didn't you get enough of a bath in the river yesterday?" Eldris teased.

I flashed him the rude hand gesture I'd wanted to give him then—two fingers raised in a V-shape.

Aristede gave a quiet huff of amusement. "Be careful what you suggest. Someone might take you up on it."

Eldris waggled his eyebrows comically. "Damn straight. Just say the word, Trouble."

Apparently rude gestures really *were* universal. Liquid heat swirled in my belly—the combination of a good stretch of deep sleep, waking curled up with Eldris, and the heart-pounding excitement of seeing the dragons up close. With that pair of suggestive comments, my body had clearly decided what sort of outlet it needed right now for the stress of the last few days.

But I still felt like I'd been trekking through the mountains for a day and a night... probably because I *had* been trekking through the mountains for a day and a night. I was pretty sure I had the brambles in my hair to prove it. I started unpicking the messy plait I'd put it in last night, teasing out the chains with their hanging gemstones as I did.

"Come bathe with me," I said casually, "and I'll let you try to convince me."

Eldris tugged his tunic over his head and *fucking hell*, if I'd known it would be that easy to get his shirt off, I would have suggested a bath in one of the disgusting little mud puddles that very first night in the desert. He was... very nice to look at.

Very, *very* nice.

"Well," he said, "what are you waiting for? Let's go!"

I blinked. *Yes*, my body seemed to say. *What are you waiting for? Let's go bathe with the pretty men who rescued you and took you to meet dragons.*

"Coming," I said a bit faintly. I cast around, seeing the saddlebags where I had stowed my meager belongings for the journey. Figuring my gems would be safer here than in my hair where they might come loose and end up at the bottom of a lake, I wrapped them in my spare tunic and stuffed them inside.

Aristede grabbed a pot of what was probably soap and a length of rough cloth to use for toweling, though I noticed he hadn't immediately started shucking clothing like Eldris had. However, his long hair had been tied back in a thong, and he did at least reach back to free it.

I took a moment to appreciate the sweep of it along his back as we headed across the valley. The two remaining horses were grazing in the far corner of the grassy space, where they had presumably escaped when the dragons appeared. I wondered if the flying beasts ever harassed them directly, or if horses were too large to be enticing prey.

Turning my attention back to Aristede, I asked, "How did you get that white streak in your hair? I don't think I've ever seen one quite like it."

"I was born with it," he said. "The skin underneath isn't quite right. It's even paler than yours."

"Not that there's anything wrong with yours," Eldris put in, clearly smug about getting one up on his friend.

Aristede shot him a quelling look. "Of course there isn't. Anyway, my mother said that even as a babe, I had a little tuft of white there. Half the people in the village thought I was cursed, and the other half thought I was blessed. My mother claims she just thought it meant I was destined to give her gray hair from an early age."

I laughed. "And did you?"

"Oh, most assuredly."

I didn't doubt that for a moment. "Well, I like it. It's distinctive."

Feeling brazen, I inserted myself between them and curled my arms through theirs.

"*Distinctive*, says the girl with blue eyes and golden hair," Eldris pointed out.

"Eh, back home, that's nothing special," I said. "Lots of blonde hair and blue eyes on the Isle of Eburos."

Eldris shrugged. "We're not on Eburos, though. Back home, I'm nothing special either."

I craned up to look at his face, my brows twitching. "That, I have a very difficult time believing."

He looked a bit pleased, and a bit sad — and for the briefest of moments, a bit lost. And in that instant, I realized that even the straightforward member of the odd trio had a past. He hadn't sprung forth, fully formed in all of his earthy, bluff good humor.

The edge of the lake spread out before us, sparkling blue in the late afternoon sun.

"The water's chilly," Aristede warned, "and the bank's a bit muddy in places. But I've never seen evidence of anything larger than a sunfish here, so it should be perfectly safe."

Eldris let my arm slip free of his and turned to me, looking down with his brow furrowed. "In all seriousness, sweet thing — are you all right with a couple of naked men splashing around with you, after… what the bandits tried to do to you on the road?"

I blinked, taken completely by surprise, and a strange, twisty feeling took up residence in my stomach.

"They didn't do anything to me," I said quickly. Maybe a bit *too* quickly.

Eldris continued to watch me carefully. "The marks I saw on your breast that day said otherwise. I just want to make sure first, that's all."

I swallowed against the ridiculous burn of tears. Where the blazes was *that* coming from? With complete honesty, I held his eyes and said, "I fail to see any connection whatsoever between that situation and this one."

"Indeed not," Aristede said from behind me. A moment later, he appeared in my line of sight. "Just be aware that both of us are old hands at buggering off when we're told to do so." He smiled, slow and dangerous. "Or doing pretty much anything else a woman tells us to do."

Holy crap. How was it possibly to go from *choked up* to *horny as fuck* in the space between one heartbeat and the next?

I scrambled for composure and raised an eyebrow, turning my attention back to Eldris. "Tell me truthfully. Have you ever in your life seen a woman tell that man to bugger off?" I asked, jerking my chin toward Aristede.

His lips twitched, covering a smile. "Not even once," he confirmed.

The grin sliding over my face was almost certainly ridiculous. I bent to hide it, pulling off my boots and stockings before shimmying out of my breeches — still stiff from drying on my body after the river crossing. Making no effort to hide myself from their gazes, I finished by stripping off the thigh-length white tunic.

"Such a pretty picture," Eldris said, once I'd thrown the light material aside. "It almost makes me feel bad about doing *this*."

Before I knew it, he'd scooped me up in tree-trunk arms and I was flying through the air with a shriek of shocked laughter, sucking in a breath before I crashed into the chilly water. I surfaced with a sputter, still laughing.

"You bastard!" I said, wiping my hair out of my face.

"No such thing as a bastard in Kulawi," he said cheerfully, peeling off his trousers to reveal... oh, my.

Oh, *my*.

SIXTEEN

I was only able to stop staring because Eldris was splashing into the lake after me with single-minded intent. I squealed like a teenage girl and shoved a wave of water toward him, at which point things immediately devolved into a vicious water fight. I only realized that Aristede had joined us when the soaking deluge aimed at me stopped abruptly, and Eldris yelped.

When I cleared my face enough to see properly, it was to find that Aristede had snuck up behind him and trapped Eldris' arms in a wrestling hold, hands laced behind his neck to lock his arms to the side.

"You sneaky..." Eldris began, twisting from one side to the other. "Whose side are you on, anyway?"

Seeing opportunity, I sucked in a quick breath and dolphin-dove, taking Eldris out at the knees. He and Aristede crashed into the water in a tangle, and all three of us surfaced a few moments later, laughing and coughing in roughly equal measure.

"Oh my gods," I said, sliding onto my back to float with my eyes closed. "I really needed this."

Someone—Eldris, I suspected—flicked water at me, but as I had known they would, the pair let me relax in the late-slanting sun, our play-feud forgotten. It was true—I needed this badly after the past few days. I didn't want to think about bandits. I didn't want to think about Prince Oblisii. I didn't want to think about Nyx disappearing into the woods. I didn't want to think about people hunting dragons. And I certainly didn't want to think about godsdamned Rayth and his godsdamned cock making me hot and needy as he pinned me after winning our sparring match.

Right now, I was swimming in a pristine mountain lake with two of the finest examples of manhood I'd come across in my twenty-two years of life. And I was going to enjoy every frigging minute of the next few hours until Rayth stumbled back to the cave and real life intruded on things once more.

I filled my lungs and twisted my body, slicing beneath the water's surface. A few strong strokes propelled me to the bank, where I climbed up just long enough to retrieve the little pot Aristede had brought. It was plain, homemade soap, not scented like the fancy goop Beshaam had used to wash me at the palace. Right now, that suited me just fine.

I waded out to a jutting boulder, the water next to it reaching my hips. Using the boulder as a shelf to hold the soap, I began lathering myself — glad to finally get rid of the travel grime. The men joined me soon after.

It was the first good look I'd gotten at Aristede, and my gaze caught on the patchwork of scars covering his upper body. Now, any man who's spent a lifetime soldiering will have scars, it was true. But his were... extensive. My eyes caught on one in particular that slashed across the base of his throat in a terrifying silver line. His penchant for high-necked tunics had hidden it from my gaze until now, and I swallowed — imagining Aristede lying on the ground, blood streaming from his neck.

A moment of dizziness assailed me.

Aristede was watching me watching him. They both were, actually. What was the appropriate thing to say in this kind of situation?

I decided on the truth. "I'm glad you survived all that. I'd've hated not getting a chance to meet you."

I lifted my eyes to his gray ones, and was rewarded with a small smile.

"More lives than a cat, that one," Eldris muttered, and I wondered if he, too, was thinking about how close Aristede must have come to death. I wondered… if he'd been there when it happened.

"I'll be the cat that got the cream, today," Aristede said lightly. "Turn around, Frella, and I'll help you wash your back."

⚜

The sun was slipping below the craggy peaks by the time we finished soaping each other and dove back into the depths to rinse off. I got the distinct impression that the art of the tease was something these two had honed and perfected over the years. It certainly seemed to be working rather effectively on me.

By the time we gathered everything up and headed back toward the cave, energy was fairly crackling between us, like the air before a thunderstorm. I'd thrown on my tunic to ward off the faint chill, and pulled my soft, knee-high riding boots back on for the walk, lacing them up sloppily. The slide of my bare thighs as I walked was almost enough to make me shiver with need at this point. I was nearly vibrating with pent-up impatience.

"Race you back!" I called, haring off at a dead run to dispel some of it.

Footsteps followed—heavy ones, probably Eldris. He was a large man, not built for speed, but short legs were short legs no matter how you looked at it, and that was what I had. There was also the matter of me not being terribly motivated to avoid getting caught. And of my feet still being sore from all the walking to get here. The practical upshot was that before we'd gone terribly far, a hand caught my shoulder and an arm wrapped around me from behind, halting my forward progress.

"I win," Eldris murmured in my ear.

Before I could formulate a reply, I was turned in his grip and slung over his broad shoulder like I weighed nothing. And trust me when I say—short girl or no—I did *not* weigh nothing. I let out a tiny *oof* noise as he settled me into place and carried me the short remaining distance to the cave. I was a bit out of breath and it wasn't the world's most comfortable position, but it did give me an absolutely *smashing* view of Eldris' muscular ass.

Watching it as he walked was kind of... hypnotic, actually. I thought about copping a feel, but I didn't want to startle him into dropping me on my head. Still, it was a *very* nice ass. I was still admiring it when my body shifted again, and he set me down neatly on my feet inside the cave.

"Let me stir up the fire and put more wood on," he said, flashing me a lazy smile. "Give Ari a moment to catch up with us."

"Ari's keeping up just fine, thank you," came a dry voice from the entrance, and I passed the smile on to him.

Unwilling to draw things out any longer, I stepped forward, until my breasts brushed Aristede's bare, scarred chest through the thin material of my tunic, and kissed him. I let the breeches drop from my loose grip, and heard the soft thump of the clay soap container landing on the towel when Aristede dropped his burdens a moment later.

Aristede let me have control of the kiss at first, taking it away bit by bit, so skillfully that I barely noticed. One moment I was kissing him, and then somehow both of his hands were tangled in my wet curls and his tongue was dueling with mine, sweeping through my mouth like hot silk.

When he eventually let me up for air, I was breathless.

"You want I should go and do the 'buggering off' routine for an hour or two, Frella?" said a low voice behind me. "Let you two have some time alone?"

I craned around, knowing how I must look with my face flushed and my lips swollen. "Why?" I asked. "Are you telling me the whole 'Oh, why didn't you wait for me to get back before fucking a woman in our room?' routine back at the Purple Cloak was a complete fabrication?"

His eyes darkened as I said the word 'fucking.'

"Not at all," he said, "but I wasn't asking for me. I was asking for you."

I raised my eyebrows. "I was raised by a handfasted triad. My brother has three lovers. And I spent most of the time while you were carrying me fighting to keep myself from grabbing your ass." I paused for a moment, thinking. "Tell you what. Do you like to watch?"

A soft breath of laughter.

"He likes to boss." Aristede's voice tickled the skin of my throat, behind my ear. His lips followed.

Eldris' grin was a slash of brilliant white in the dimming light. "Only because you seem to enjoy it so much."

I caught Aristede's careless shrug from the corner of my eye. "I never said he was bad at it," he confided into my ear, and my heart picked up its tripping pace.

I smiled. "Fair enough. All right, big man, tell us what to do." Practicality reared its unwelcome head, and I sobered for a moment. "Just... don't come inside me. That goes for both of you."

Aristede pulled back, his face becoming serious. "We won't, Frella. Our word. There are other ways to enjoy each other, and I promise that neither of us have left a trail of fatherless children in our wake."

I relaxed, the smile returning to my face. "Good answer. Now, where were we?"

"Hmm," Eldris mused. "I think you were just about to relieve Ari of his trousers and smallclothes."

"You know," I agreed, "I think you're absolutely right."

I suited word to deed, pausing to help him remove his boots. The fire was crackling higher now that Eldris had put more wood on it, throwing a warm orange glow around the cave as the sun disappeared outside. I crouched before Aristede's freshly bared form, admiring my handiwork.

The scars crisscrossing his body did nothing to detract from his beauty; they merely gave it a bittersweet edge. *Appreciate this man*, they said. *He so easily might not be here at all.* His was not the powerful build of Eldris, or the hard sinew of Rayth. Aristede was all graceful planes and curves—a sculptor's masterpiece come to life, marred here and there by a slip of the chisel in a moment of too much passion.

His hair fascinated me, and not just for its streak of white. It fell to the small of his back, straight and blunt-cut at the bottom, as though if he didn't lop it off every once in a while, it would keep growing and growing until he tripped on it. By contrast, my unruly curls grew to about mid-back and no further.

Just as intriguing, his hair never seemed to tangle. Even after more than a day of rough travel… even wet from a dip in the lake, it hung in a smooth, silken wave. My fingers itched to run through the drying strands, but before they could, Eldris spoke again.

"Your turn now, sweet thing. Let us see those pretty curves."

Aristede's smile tilted up. Warmth spread through me, and I moved to unlace my boots.

"Nah," Eldris said. "Leave those on."

The warmth turned to fiery heat, but I managed not to make any embarrassing noises as I halted my abortive attempt to remove the knee-high boots. Instead, I stood and stripped off the tunic, tossing it aside carelessly. I turned until I could see both men, reveling in the appreciative looks they were giving me. Standing here in my tall boots made me feel oddly powerful, and I decided I liked it.

I liked it *a lot*.

Eldris had made himself comfortable on one of the bedrolls and unlaced his breeches, freeing his rather impressive length. He lounged on an elbow, amusement tugging at his features. "Well, go on," he said. "Kiss him again. Muss 'im up a bit—we both know you want to."

Maybe I'd spoken too soon when I failed to lump Eldris in with the others as dangerous. He saw too much. He also had good ideas, though, so my reassessment of his character could probably wait for some time when my sex wasn't throbbing and dripping down my inner thighs.

I kissed Aristede. I also gave into the urge to run my hands through that silky hair. Aristede hadn't exactly been shy about returning the gesture before, but this time he wound my tangled mass of curls around his fingers and used it to tug my head back, exposing the column of my throat to his lips and teeth.

My thighs got wetter. My nipples got harder, but at least I could rub those against his chest to get some relief.

"Is she dripping for you yet, Ari?" Eldris asked.

The hand not fisted in my hair skimmed down my ribs and over my hip, leaving heat in its wake. Aristede brushed fingertips over the globe of my ass and stroked down the length of the valley running between my buttocks, delving low to find the evidence of my arousal.

"Completely soaked," Aristede confirmed. "Though I'm not sure it's just for me."

"It's not," I admitted breathlessly. "Eldris, you're secretly evil and I think I love you."

Eldris chuckled. "Tell me that again after we're both done with you tonight."

"*Nngh*," I managed, as Aristede's fingers appeared to seek more detailed information about the source of my slickness.

"Oh, yeah," Eldris said. "This is gonna be fun."

Aristede smiled through the final kiss he pressed to my lips before letting his hands slide out of my hair and my sex. My scalp tingled from his grip—but then, so did everything else. He drew me down on the other bedroll, lying on his back and urging me to straddle his chest. I wasn't sure what he was after until he nudged me higher up his body and stretched his arms over his head, out of the way of my knees.

Heart pounding, I brushed the lips of my sex across the bow of his mouth, like it was another kiss. Mostly, I'd gravitated toward the tough boys back in Eburos. Apprentice warriors, and the like. Many of them had been happy to lay me down on my back, spread my legs, and eat me out. Several had even been good at it. But the feeling of kneeling over a prone lover in my leather boots and… *using* him like this, especially while another man watched…

I really, *really* liked it.

"Don't let her come," Eldris said. I jerked my head around to pin him with a glare of disbelief, but he only smirked at me. "What's that look for, Trouble? The anticipation's half the fun."

I drew a breath to tell him what I thought of that opinion, but Aristede was taking control of my sex the same way he'd taken control of the kiss earlier. All that came out was a pathetic little whining noise.

"Yeah… I thought so," Eldris said with satisfaction. I clamped my lips together and settled for glaring at him some more.

Aristede's tongue was diabolical, and not just for its facile way with words. I decided that no one had any right to know my body this well without any prior sexual history with me. He lapped and delved, circling sensitive flesh, teasing with the promise of more but never quite delivering.

My breath was coming in ragged pants when Eldris asked, "You enjoy sucking a man's cock, sweet thing?"

"Love it," I gasped, shivering as Aristede's tongue flicked over my most sensitive place, only to retreat.

"Why don't you turn around and get your revenge on him while he's working on you?" he suggested. "See how close to the edge you can get him without letting him come."

Revenge—yeah, I liked the sound of that. I clambered around on shaky knees, happy for the excuse to fall forward and brace myself on all fours. Balance was a lot easier when your head wasn't spinning from frustrated lust.

Aristede's cock was as beautiful as the rest of him, jutting hard and proud, leaking milky seed from the tip in a thin stream. I hadn't touched him yet; this was all from kissing me and letting me ride his talented mouth. Was it also from Eldris? From his eyes on us, and the fond, lazy amusement behind his orders? Were they lovers, or merely close friends?

My moment of coherent thought was interrupted by another slow flick of Aristede's tongue. He nuzzled at me, a low, male noise vibrating against sensitive flesh. I had to fight the urge to swallow down that pretty cock and hollow my cheeks until he spilled down my throat, but what he was doing to me definitely deserved some payback first.

I contented myself with light kisses and licks, lapping up the mess he was making of himself… following the trail to its source and delving into the slit in pursuit of that salty bitterness. We silently dared each other to get closer to release without slipping over the edge, our noises growing more desperate... hungrier.

I drew more of him into my mouth. He retaliated by curling his tongue inside my passage. I sucked. He nipped. I set up a slow rhythm, only to break it when his hips began to flex up beneath me. He drew back to blow cool air over my soaked folds.

There was no telling how long we might have been able to keep it up, had I not made the mistake of throwing Eldris a sideways look that I'd intended to be sultry. He hadn't moved from his relaxed slouch on the blankets, but now he was fisting his generous cock with unhurried strokes as he watched the show we were putting on. His eyes met mine, dark and heavy-lidded.

I groaned around the slick flesh in my mouth and came hard, days of pent-up tension exploding in a blaze of sensation that wracked me to the bone. This was apparently too much for Aristede, who arched and spurted his release across my tongue. I swallowed and jerked against his mouth and swallowed some more, only vaguely aware of my surroundings beyond those two incandescent points of contact.

When I came back to myself, I was still sprawled inelegantly on Aristede's spent body — probably smothering him with my quivering sex. Not that he seemed to be complaining... though I had a moment's worry that the lack of protest meant I'd already rendered him unconscious. To be safe, I slithered to one side, my body feeling as weak and uncoordinated as a newborn lamb's.

I ended up face-down in the blankets, and would have stayed that way if not for the strong hands that rearranged me onto my back with my head and shoulders resting on Aristede's torso, my body lying perpendicular to his. My human pillow wrapped an arm around me loosely, his hand splayed over my left breast.

"All warmed up now?" Eldris asked, making space for himself between my spread legs. His large, callused hand rested on my belly for a moment before sliding down to cup my sex.

I shuddered as a little aftershock shot through me. "Uh-huh," I said faintly, still floating happily in la-la land.

"Glad to hear it," Eldris said, clearly amused at my expense.

I wrinkled my nose at him, but the witty rejoinder I was crafting dissolved into a moan of pleasure as two thick fingers slid inside me. Fucking *gods*. There was nothing quite like the first stretch of penetration. For that, a tongue just wasn't enough.

Aristede's clever fingers worried my nipple, somehow intuiting my preference for an edge of pain at the turgid peak. I melted between them, letting the sensations flow through me.

"Wrists?" Eldris said, and I was confused for a moment until Aristede gathered my hands, holding them stretched above my head in one of his. "Let us know if any of this isn't doing it for you, sweet thing."

"Mmnh," I groaned, melting anew as Aristede returned his free hand to torturing my erect nipples.

Eldris crooked his fingers, sliding back and forth against the front wall of my passage. His thumb slid across my oversensitive nub with every stroke, while another finger tickled across my ass. I writhed, testing Aristede's grip as my lethargic heart dragged itself back to a thundering rhythm.

"*Utarr's dripping tits,*" I cursed as Eldris expertly pushed me to a second climax in almost no time at all. "What—*ah!* What happened to 'anticipation is half of the fun?'"

Eldris grinned. "Well… that was as much for Ari's benefit as yours." His fingers slid over the place inside of me, picking up the same inexorable rhythm as before. "And besides… now you can anticipate the fact that I don't plan on stopping this anytime soon."

SEVENTEEN

Eldris, it turned out, was a patient man. A patient, diabolical, unexpectedly *sadistic* man. Silly me, I had previously been unaware of the lengths to which my body could be pushed without breaking completely. I'd also never screamed during sex before.

"Let us hear that voice, sweet thing," Eldris said, at some point after I'd lost track of the number of climaxes he'd wrenched from me.

I was pretty sure there was a finger inside my ass now, too, and Aristede had started splitting his time between teasing my breasts and sliding his long fingers between my lips, fucking my mouth with deep strokes.

"No one around to hear if you do," Aristede observed, trailing wet fingers back down to my breasts. "At least, not unless Rayth wanders back here at an inopportune moment."

Godsdamn my twisted, sex-drugged mind—somehow, the vision of Rayth walking in on me writhing between these two, every opening filled, was enough to tighten all the muscles in my body into immobility as a full-throated scream of release tore free of my lungs.

I... might've blacked out afterward. Just, y'know, *a bit*.

When I came back from the thing that... might've been a blackout, it was to the heavenly sensation of fingertips stroking my forehead and temple, while soft lips pressed delicate kisses to the knuckles of my right hand.

I smiled, not opening my eyes.

"There she is," Eldris said warmly. "All good, sweetheart?"

"Really, really good," I slurred. A thought struggled free of the morass in my brain, and I peeled open one eye to look up at him. "Did you come, too?"

He smiled. "Not yet. I can finish myself, if you like. Or, if it's all right, you can lie back right where you are and I'll have the space between these two lovely flotation aides of yours." He tweaked a nipple, sending a pleasant flush of warmth through me.

"All yours," I said sleepily, settling my head more comfortably against Aristede's taut stomach.

Lips brushed mine, fuller and softer than Aristede's.

"You're just perfect, sweet thing," Eldris said.

"I thought I was *trouble*," I teased.

"Definitely that, too," he agreed.

Aristede gathered my hair and draped it across his stomach, presumably to keep it out of the way when Eldris spilled all over me. *That was nice*, I thought. There was something about a man spurting hot seed across my skin that did it for me, but it would be a mess to clean out of my hair afterward.

Eldris mounted without so much as jostling me, muscular thighs bracketing my ribcage. I dragged heavy eyelids open, not wanting to miss the sight of him looming over me, his big cock throbbing as he kneaded and molded my breasts together to take his length between them.

"Beautiful," he said, as the slick head of his prick slid between the twin mounds.

"You, too," I said dreamily. "Both of you."

I slipped peacefully into the rhythm of his easy thrusts, enjoying the warm weight of his hands cupping my breasts together to make a hot, tight space for himself. He took his time, enjoying himself without drawing things out unnecessarily, and I hummed in satisfaction when ropes of hot seed slapped against my chest, neck, and chin.

Eldris breathed raggedly, but didn't let his weight sag down onto me. When his shudders stilled, he moved off of my body. I sighed in complete relaxation and swiped the smear of come off my chin with a finger, popping it into my mouth so I'd be able to say I'd tasted both of them.

"*Goddess*," Eldris breathed.

"Towel," Aristede said, his voice amused, and I might have laughed if that didn't sound like far too much work.

A moment later, the damp towel we'd used at the lake swiped at my chest and throat, then between my legs, where I'd made a truly epic—and thoroughly enjoyable—mess of myself. Afterward, strong arms shuffled me around, rearranging blankets and bed-mats until I was cradled between two warm bodies in a comfortable nest. A few heartbeats later, I was fast asleep, dead to the world.

When I awoke, it was light outside. Also, Rayth was standing next to the bedroll, staring down at the three of us with his arm out of its sling and an unimpressed expression gracing his haughty features. Overall, it wasn't nearly as enjoyable an experience as my sex-addled mind had insisted last night that it would be.

Eldris was awake, but hadn't bothered to move from our pleasant tangle of limbs. "Problem?" he asked mildly, though I thought I detected an edge beneath the friendly tone.

"*Problem*," Rayth echoed in a flat voice. "Are you fucking joking with me right now?"

He nudged Aristede awake with the toe of his boot—not gently. I bristled upon realizing that many hours had obviously passed, and Aristede had been peacefully asleep the whole time, evidently untroubled by nightmares until Rayth jammed a foot into his ribs and ruined it. He snorted awake, startled but not flailing, his expression groggy and his appearance pleasingly rumpled.

All three of us were as naked as the day we'd been born… not that I liked to think too much about the day I'd been born, since that day had also marked my mother's death. Still, my nakedness was all that kept me from leaping up to get in Rayth's face and tell him not to be such an asshole.

"What. The *hell*. Were you *thinking*?" Rayth growled as Aristede blinked up at him. "I'm aware that your first reaction to anything with a heartbeat is 'can I have sex with it,' but in *what conceivable realm* was this a good idea? You're the one who claimed she's bonding with the white dragon. If I'm to be saddled with this hellion, I sure as fuck don't need her pining after *you* once she realizes what a shameless man-whore you are!"

My mouth was hanging open. I snapped it shut and scrambled to my feet, heedless of my lack of clothing. Rayth's eyes trailed down my body. I realized that I'd been wrong earlier—I wasn't as naked as the day I'd been born. I still had the tall leather boots on.

I poked Rayth in the chest. "Eyes up here, asshole," I snapped. "Where the hell do you get off—"

"*Frella.*" Aristede's voice was firm. "Leave it. This is an old argument, and one that won't be won today. Besides, he has a point. It may have been... unwise... for us to indulge as we did."

I whirled to stare at him instead of Rayth, hurt starting to bleed in around the outrage. Of course, that was enough to immediately put me on the offensive. "*Excuse* me? Maybe I just wanted a casual roll in the blankets, did you ever think of that? You have a pretty face, and you damn well know it. I'd been looking for an excuse to tumble you into bed since I first saw you. Last night was as good of one as any. That's all it was, so *get over yourself.*"

There was the strangest tangle of relief and disquiet in Aristede's eyes, but I was too angry right now to parse it. *Angry.* Not hurt.

Damn it.

"I need to get out of here," I muttered, scavenging for my discarded clothing and tugging my tunic on with sharp movements. I cast around for some excuse. "Maybe I'll... go look for the white dragon again."

Eldris rose, unconcerned by his nudity. "I'll come with you. We'll take my horse." He gathered his own clothing and straightened, turning to Rayth, who still looked incandescent with anger. "You an' me... we'll talk later." The words emerged hard.

"Yes," Rayth said. "We will. Maybe we can talk about your obvious attempt at misdirection yesterday, which might have been more effective if the hellion hadn't carved markings along the trail as she went."

"Sure, we can talk about that," Eldris agreed, not rising to the bait as he pulled on his trousers. "C'mon, sweet thing. Let's go saddle up and take a ride."

"Wait." I balked, a chill creeping in as I realized Rayth had found the right trail after all, rather than wandering around on a completely different part of the mountain than where Nyx had disappeared. "Nyx. Did you find him? Is he—"

"No," Rayth said flatly. "I didn't find him. If there's one thing young Leannyck has always been good at, it's running away and hiding in the bushes like a frightened rabbit."

"Fuck you, Rayth," I spat.

He stared at me coldly. "I believe there's been more than enough of that already."

I'm not… entirely sure what I would have said or done next, but—perhaps fortunately—Eldris' hand closed around my upper arm before I could do anything but sputter.

"Frella." His rumbling voice was uncharacteristically quiet. "Let's go."

I let him guide me outside, and didn't speak to him as we dressed the rest of the way. The saddles were stored under a rocky overhang near the cave entrance, and he retrieved his tack, slinging it under a beefy arm. He allowed the silence to settle around us, taking a circuitous route through the valley that led past some berry bushes.

The fruit was just starting to ripen, but there was enough for us to call it breakfast. I barely tasted the little red spheres, eating only because I knew I needed to keep my strength up. Afterward, we skirted the edge of the lake and drank from the clear spring that flowed into it. I tried not to think about the events of the previous afternoon as my eyes strayed over the sparkling body of water where we'd laughed and played like teenagers.

Eldris retrieved his horse from the grassy field and tacked up the big chestnut gelding. He mounted and helped me swing up behind him. Only when we were wandering across the valley at a sedate walk, my arms wrapped around his waist, did he break the silence.

"Where do you want to go?" he asked.

"To the trail I marked," I said, after a moment's hesitation. "That's where I first saw the white dragon." *And where I last saw Nyx*, I didn't add.

"Sure. Makes sense," he agreed easily, and reined the gelding in that direction.

We fell quiet again for several minutes, the trees closing around us as we entered the trailhead.

"What the hell is Rayth's problem?" I asked eventually.

Eldris seemed to consider his words. "He's worried about the dragons. We blindsided him with that news about you and the white male, and now he has to worry about how you being here will affect the group."

I shook my head. "No. Well, maybe so—but it's more than that. He's disliked me from the moment we first met."

Another pause.

"There was… a woman. He loved her, and she betrayed him." I waited for Eldris to elaborate, but he only sighed into the expectant silence. "That's all I know, Frella. He never talks about his past. At least, not when he's sober."

I swallowed the barb that wanted to rise. *And when is that, exactly?* It wasn't helpful, and I knew it.

"So now all women are automatically suspect?" I asked instead, letting the tartness come through in my voice.

"Only the ones he's attracted to, I expect."

And, oh *hell*, no. We were *not* going there right now. We weren't going there *ever*, if I had anything to say about it.

I changed the subject gracelessly. "Are you and Aristede lovers?"

"No," he said immediately.

"Why not?" I asked.

There was a beat of thoughtful silence. "Because I value his friendship too much."

"So, that means you'd *like* to be," I mused. "I thought so."

Eldris didn't stiffen under my arms, and his tone wasn't angry when he replied. It was cautious, though. "What makes you say that?"

I shrugged, leaning against his broad back as the horse picked its way down the narrow trail. "You were using my body as an extension of yours last night. Telling me how to touch him. How to please him." I thought back to our evening of debauchery, shivering a bit. "And when I looked over and saw you pleasuring yourself as you watched it, I didn't think it was just me you were looking at."

He nodded, and for the first time I wished I could see his face as we talked.

"Does it bother you?" he asked.

My brows drew together. "Why would it?"

"Northerners have got some really strange ideas about men and women enjoying each other, and you're more northern than most, sweet thing."

"Oh." It was true enough—just not in my particular case. "No… you're right. Some of them do. But I was raised by a man, a eunuch, and

someone with a female body who lives as male —
and they all love each other. Two of my brother's
three lovers are men. To me, it's normal. It's just
love."

"Just love," he echoed. "I like that."

"Why do you say you value Aristede's
friendship too much to become his lover?" I
prodded. "Would the idea offend him?"

I felt Eldris' breath of laughter through my
grip on his waist. "Not hardly. Rayth wasn't far off
that he'll sleep with anyone that'll have him. I think
it helps keep his nightmares at bay. But… he never
fucks the same person twice." His voice lowered to
a barely audible mutter. "'Cause if he did, then
they might start to get a glimpse of what's hidden
behind those walls."

I'd intended to ask more about those
nightmares; to see if Eldris was willing to let
anything else slip. But then the next words he'd
said stopped me cold.

He never fucks the same person twice.

*I don't need her pining after you once she realizes
what a shameless man-whore you are.*

Rayth's reaction fell into place like the pieces
of a child's wooden puzzle. I stiffened, but kept my
voice carefully neutral as I replied.

"And neither of you thought this might be
relevant information for me to have yesterday
evening?"

His chest rose and fell heavily. "I doubt it even
occurred to him. It's just not how his mind works.
And I thought…"

"You thought *what*?" I pressed.

He sighed again. "I thought you might be the woman to show him a better way. I still think that."

I pondered his words. "You should have talked to me first."

"Yeah."

Silence fell again as we reached the clearing where I'd seen the male dragon. It was quiet but for the wind rustling through the leaves and the sounds of small birds. I took a deep, cleansing breath and let it out slowly.

"There's nothing here," I said. "Let's go back, I guess."

We turned and headed back the way we'd come, the atmosphere around us heavy. Eldris was the one to breach it as we approached the trailhead and the valley beyond.

"For what it's worth, Frella, I don't drop people so easily. Not unless they want me to." He swallowed hard. "I've no idea if you're even interested in me after this morning's shitshow. But I care for you. The two of us... we fit. If you want me to fuck you to sleep every night, I will. If you want me to hold you in my arms and stroke your hair, I will. If you want me to bugger off, I'll do that. But unless you tell me to my face that you no longer want me around at all... I'll keep coming back, afterward."

An unexpected lump rose in my throat, a choking noise emerging from my lips instead of words. Tears burned at the backs of my eyes. *Naloth's balls*, what the hell was *wrong* with me these days?

Since I couldn't seem to speak, I squeezed my arms hard around Eldris' body instead. This turned out to be a good plan, since the horse chose that moment to spook violently sideways, very nearly managing to scrape us off on an unfortunately placed tree.

I yelped, clinging to Eldris and gripping with my knees as he wrestled with the reins.

"*Whoa*," Eldris growled, dragging the gelding back under control. "What the hell?"

He helped me dismount and followed me down, holding the gelding on a close rein as the animal danced sideways and snorted. I retraced our steps toward the trailhead, Eldris coaxing the horse forward as he followed behind me. My hand strayed to my knife-belt, grasping the hilt of one of the throwing knives in readiness.

I emerged into the grassy valley, only to come face to face with an unexpected sight. Perhaps two dozen paces away, Nyx stood frozen, supporting the broken wing of a small dragon with blood smeared across its hide.

I gaped at Nyx, and he gaped at me. I was only vaguely aware of Eldris arriving at my shoulder with his nervous horse in tow, as I tried to make sense of the scene. The dragon was noticeably shorter and lighter than the others I'd seen, its ribs and shoulder blades standing out starkly under its hide. Its scales were coming in green around the head, but they, too, seemed dull rather than lustrous.

The damaged wing had a horrible, blood-crusted tear through the webbing, and some of the delicate bones looked wrong. Broken. The dragon was limping, the side of her body with the injured wing showing evidence of deep cuts and scrapes on the tough skin. Her head hung low, but her emerald eyes blazed.

My gaze flew to Nyx, and I gasped. Those multi-colored hazel eyes I'd so admired shone with the same eerie inner light, the green swallowing the brown. He looked... feverish. Enflamed.

Unearthly.

"Please," he said. "I know if I go back to the cave, Prince Rathanii will kill me. But... I can feel the dragon, like she's inside my mind somehow. She's badly hurt. She needs help, and I refuse to let her die."

I looked at Eldris, wide-eyed, the implications crashing down on me like an avalanche. The man Rayth wanted to kill had just formed a soul-bond with one of his beloved dragons. The wine-soaked bastard should have counted himself lucky when he walked in to find Eldris and Aristede in bed with me. He didn't know when he was well off. And... *Prince Rathanii*? What was *that* about?

For a moment, Eldris looked like he was at as much of a loss as I was. He recovered first, though, his face hardening into lines that said anyone who got in his way was about to be in for a bad time.

"You leave Rayth to me, lad," he said, his voice stony. "We'll help you get her back to the cave. No one's going to be dying today."

finis

Frella's adventures continue in *The Dragon Mistress: Book 2.*

For more books by this author, visit
www.rasteffan.com

9 781955 073547